SHOWDOWN AT PARSON'S END

When Anthony Armstrong returns to his hometown of Parson's End after completing his studies at Harvard, he expects to spend a few quiet weeks lending a hand at his family's farm. When his father is shot, however, he is drawn into a vicious range war. Armstrong longs to return to his studies, but as the body count rises, his chances of ever seeing Harvard again grow fewer by the hour. Matters reach a shattering climax when he is confronted by a ruthless and bloodthirsty band of comancheros.

THE BOOT HILL BREED

Ned Oaks

Jack Marric is returning to his family home after learning of his mother's illness. But a decision to stop for a drink at a saloon results in him getting into a fight with and killing two men who are bullying the elderly saloon-keeper. Jack is enthusiastically welcomed home by his family, but unbeknown to him, he has been followed by the brother of the two dead men, who is now hell-bent on revenge and will kill anyone who gets in his way. Soon the whole family are under threat because of Jack's act of courage . . .

BLOOD OVER BLACK CREEK

Edwin Derek

Hoping to put his violent past behind him, Matt Crowe purchases the Texas ranch of Black Creek. It has water in abundance; but at the massive and powerful neighbouring Bar-T, the waters run dry in the summer. Protected by gunmen, its hands constantly drive herds across Black Creek range to the water-rich creek that gives the ranch its name. What can one man and two beautiful young women do against the twenty hired gunmen of the mighty Bar-T? Very little, until Crowe makes a dangerous ally of an old foe . . .

SIMON WEBB

SHOWDOWN AT PARSON'S END

Complete and Unabridged

LINFORD
Leicester

First published in Great Britain in 2016 by
Robert Hale
An imprint of The Crowood Press
Wiltshire

First Linford Edition
published 2018
by arrangement with
The Crowood Press
Wiltshire

A catalogue record for this book is available
from the British Library.

ISBN 978–1–4448–3918–0

Published by
F. A. Thorpe (Publishing)
Anstey, Leicestershire

Set by Words & Graphics Ltd.
Anstey, Leicestershire
Printed and bound in Great Britain by
T. J. International Ltd., Padstow, Cornwall

This book is printed on acid-free paper

1

The scarlet mail-coach came bowling down the hill at a fair lick, coming at last within sight of its latest destination. The messenger sitting beside the driver turned round and banged on the roof with a chunk of wood, hollering, 'Parson's End. Parson's End, a-comin' up.'

Truth to tell, the messenger might as well have saved his breath, for the coach contained only a single passenger and he knew better than any employee of the stagecoach company that they were about to pull into the little town of Parson's End. After all, he had been born and raised not five miles from there and was tolerably familiar with every crack in the boardwalk on Main Street. Anthony Armstrong craned his head out of the window and watched as they entered the environs of what, he felt, had to be one of the most dreary and least interesting towns in the whole of the United States.

The first structure of note to meet his eyes was the imposing bulk of a three-storey, faded clapboard building with 'MERCHANTS HOTEL' painted on the front in letters six feet high. The absence of a possessive apostrophe, which he had never before noticed, irritated the young man. Next was a row of run-down stores, which were little better than adobe shacks with false fronts. These were emblazoned with the names of the proprietors and type of goods on offer within: THOS KIRBY, BANKER, G.M. HOOVER, LIQUOR & CIGARS, COVENEY, SUPPLIERS OF DRY GOODS, TINWARE AND GUNS. Apparently nothing at all had changed in the year and a half that he had been away and this fact too caused Armstrong to click his tongue in an expression of dissatisfaction and annoyance. The damned place hadn't changed since he was a boy. For somebody who had spent the last eighteen months at Harvard Law School, the parochialism of his home town stood out in sharp contrast to the urbanity and sophistication of Massachusetts. Had it not been for his mother's entreaties in the letters which she had been sending him every week since he went off to take up his place at college, Anthony Armstrong seriously doubted if he ever would have wished to return. Still, he thought, as the stage shuddered to a halt with a screeching of iron brakes, there it was. He was back now for the Hilary vacation and might just as well make the best of it.

It did not strike Armstrong, until he had left the stage and was walking along the wooden sidewalk towards the track which would lead him to his parents' home, that he was dressed any differently from other folk in the town. But then, since he had begun at Harvard, he had grown so used to wearing sober, semi-clerical black suits that he had donned one for the journey home without thinking anything of it. The boot boy at the hotel where he had stayed a couple of nights back had polished his black shoes until they shone like looking-glasses. His attention was drawn to the matter as he passed the Lucky Lady and one of a pair of loafers, standing near the entrance to the bar, remarked, 'Hooee, looks like a damn woman, with them shiny shoes. Howdy, lil' lady!'

Being slightly built and shorter than average, Anthony Armstrong was quite used to fellows like this; men who thought to make him the butt of their pleasantries. He walked over to the scruffy, mean-looking men and asked amiably, 'Would you care to repeat that?'

The two loafers, both aged about thirty or thereabouts, exchanged glances and one winked at his partner, before saying, 'I was just admirin' your shoe-leather is all. That and 'markin' as them shoes'd look more fittin' on a woman's feet than a man's.'

The words were scarcely out of the fellow's mouth, before Armstrong delivered a ferocious punch to his chin, sending him sprawling across the sidewalk. It was not the first time in his life that foolish people had thought that Anthony Armstrong's modest size and quiet demeanour indicated that he was a soft mark. He was, however, a leading light in the Harvard Boxing Club and had never in all his life allowed anybody to make game of him. While he was waiting for the man whom he had knocked down to rise and set to with him, the batwing doors of the saloon swung open and an elderly man with a bristling, iron-grey moustache strode out. Catching sight of the fellow lying on the sidewalk, clutching his jaw tenderly, the newcomer said sharply, 'I don't pay you boys good money to start brawling in the street like guttersnipes as soon as I turn my back on you! What d'you mean by it? Get up this minute.' Then he caught sight of Anthony Armstrong, standing at his ease and waiting to see how the fight which he had initiated might develop. The older man looked at him a little uncertainly, before saying, 'Anthony. Back in town, hey?'

'Yes, sir.' It was an embarrassing circumstance, because he and his family had been, and for aught he knew to the contrary still were, at outs with Michael Doolan and his boys. Not but that they hadn't got on well enough with them until a couple of years back, but things had become mighty sour before he'd left for Harvard and he didn't rightly know which way the wind was currently blowing.

'Well,' said Mr Doolan, 'happen I'll see you about in town.'

'How's your daughter, sir?'

'Which one of 'em?'

'Katy.'

'She's well enough. Why d'you ask?'

'Oh, no particular reason.'

Michael Doolan stared at Anthony for a few seconds, as though he might have something more to say. Then he turned to the fellow that Anthony had punched and said gruffly, 'Get up, Hogan. Less'n you're wanting to see your wages docked. We got work to do.'

Before he got to his feet and followed his boss, the man called Hogan favoured Armstrong with an evil glare, which suggested that if they met again, then there were apt to be fireworks.

The town of Parson's End contained something in the region of six hundred souls when young Anthony Armstrong came in on the mail coach that day in the spring of 1867. The settlement had grown up at a ford across a tributary of the Legrande River, which wended its way through the Tonto Basin. The river-crossing had already been known as Parson's End some years before the first buildings had been erected on the spot that would later form the nucleus of the new town. Almost fifty years earlier, in the late summer of 1819, a Presbyterian missioner had been making his way through the valley on the way to the Lord only knew where. For some reason or another, the local Navajo Indians were feeling a mite ticked off with white men just then and had seized the minister and lashed his ankles and wrists to four stout wooden stakes which they had driven into the ground by the ford. Then they had carefully removed his eyelids with a razor-sharp hunting knife and left him facing the sun. It was supposed by those who came upon his remains three days later that the sun would have blinded him before he had died of thirst. There were those who said that the minister's sightless ghost haunted the road thereabouts on the anniversary of his death. Some wag had soon after christened the location Parson's End and the name had stuck.

Before the town had sprung up, men had come to this part of the Arizona Territory, hoping to make their fortunes. Those who had succeeded in doing so were few and far between, but Seth Armstrong, Anthony's father, had been one of them. He now owned, or lay claim to, half of the land between the Legrande and the boundary of the Arizona Territory to the north of it. On the other side of the river, Michael

Doolan and his clan held sway.

Although the Armstrongs and Doolans were by far and away the biggest landowners in this part of Arizona, their spreads were surrounded on all sides by other, smaller concerns. Since the feud had arisen between the two families, the men farming the land near to them tended to take sides, looking for protection from one or the other of the two powerful families in the valley. That, at any rate, had been the state of affairs for some while before Anthony Armstrong had left Arizona and headed East. It remained to be seen how things were currently situated.

He wondered if Katy had forgotten him now. The summer before last, they had enjoyed a flirtation; all the more exciting for being undertaken secretly, in flat opposition to the wishes of both their families. For Anthony, though, it had been a little more than just a game. He still believed himself to be in love with Katy Doolan.

It was a fine enough day and since he

was burdened only with an old carpet bag, young Armstrong made good time, coming in sight of his home in under two hours. The farmhouse that his father had built before going in search of a bride had been added to and embellished over the thirty-two years since Martha Armstrong had somehow been persuaded to leave the civilized country in the East and come out to settle in the wilderness. Much had changed in the district since then and there were hopes that before too much longer Arizona would be admitted as a new state of the Union. True, the territory had technically been on the side of the Confederacy during the late War Between the States, but there was no sign that Washington held that against them. Besides, it was a debatable point where the true allegiance of most of those living in Arizona had actually lain. After all, many of them, Anthony Armstrong included, had fought for the Union, rather than for the Confederacy.

His mother was the first to see him. She was harvesting some herbs from the vegetable garden at back of the house, which was her pride, and chanced to look up and see her youngest son bearing down upon her. It was not in Martha Armstrong's nature to show too much of her real feelings and emotions and so she contented herself with saying in a gruff tone of voice, 'You surely took your time. I been expecting you since these three days gone. What kept you?' Then, because Anthony was her youngest son and also her favourite child, she was unable to maintain the pretence any longer and hurried up to embrace him. 'You stayed away too long,' she told him, 'You hear what I tell you?'

'Sure, Ma. I'm sorry. I won't leave it so long next time.'

Martha Armstrong stood back from her beloved youngest son and looked him over carefully. Although she was hugely proud of the boy and secretly impressed with his smart appearance, she didn't wish to let him know so and therefore said, 'I hope them fine clothes don't mean you think you're too good to help out round the place over the Eastertide? There's a heap o' work to be done.'

'I'm no prouder now than when I set off to Harvard,' replied her son, stung a little by the suggestion that he might have changed. 'I can still feed hogs or plough a furrow if need be and do it as good as those brothers of mine, as well you know.'

'Well well, we'll see. It's good to have you home again. Come and set in the kitchen now and have a bite to eat.'

Although they had not seen their little brother for over a year, his brothers Tom, Jack and Andrew, greeted Anthony with the same casual and good-natured contempt that they always had done. They none of them inquired about his life at college, but instead said things like, 'Looky here, the scholar's come to see us!' and 'Lord, who set that tailor's dummy at table?'

'What are you rascals up to these days?' asked Anthony. 'I saw Mr Doolan in town, but he didn't seem overly keen to stop and talk with me.'

'That whoreson — ' muttered Jack and then jerked back in pain as his mother turned from the stove and rapped his head smartly with the ladle with which she had been stirring the pot of soup.

'You mind your mouth when you're in my kitchen,' she said, 'I'll not have a heap of cursing and dirty talk at table.'

Martha Armstrong ruled her house with a rod of iron and this had not changed as her sons grew to manhood. Jack was twenty-eight, but he still deferred to his mother as he had done since he was knee-high to a grasshopper. The three sons who still lived with her might be regular terrors when they were out on the range or raising Cain in a saloon, but indoors, under the strict eye of their indomitable mother, they behaved like Sunday school pupils.

Seth Armstrong came in a little after

his sons and he greeted his youngest boy with the same casual air, as though he might have seen him at breakfast that day. Like the rest of the family, he wasn't a whale at showing his feelings. 'Ah, you're back, then? Reckon you'll be any help around the place? Those brothers of yours aren't worth sh — a cuss when it comes to good, honest work.'

'Sure I can help out, Pa. What's doing these days?'

'No talkin' business at table,' said his mother firmly. 'Let's converse of more pleasant topics, like how you're doing in your studies.'

After Anthony had sketched out his progress in qualifying as a lawyer, explaining about the difference between criminal law and the civil law or torts, he said, 'Had a run-in with one of Mr Doolan's fellows earlier.'

'The hell you did!' said Tom and then, as his mother glared at him, added hastily, 'Sorry, Ma. It just slipped out.'

'What chanced, son?' asked Seth.

After Anthony had given a brief account of the incident outside the Lucky Lady, there was a sombre silence. Tom said, 'You say his name was Hogan? I know him. He's one o' them — ' He stopped dead at a sharp and imperious gesture from his father.

'You mind your mother now,' said Seth Armstrong, 'You heard what she told you. No talking business at table. Tell us some more about these here 'torts', Anthony. It sounds right interestin'!'

'Torts!' muttered Tom quietly, 'sounds like Mexican vittles or somethin'.'

Throughout the meal, Anthony could not help but notice that his father seemed a little vague. It was nothing to put one's finger on, but just that he had to say some things twice before the old man appeared fully to apprehend his meaning. It was a mite troubling and he made sure to ask his brothers later about it. After they had finished the soup and bread, Seth asked his youngest son to come for a walk around the place. To his three elder sons, he said, 'You boys know what's needful. Just be carryin' on with it.'

If anybody knew that Anthony Armstrong was no soft body or weakling, it was his father. However much his brothers chaffed him, Seth knew that his youngest boy had more about him than any of them guessed. When all was said and done, Anthony had been to war and that was something he had in common with his father, who had himself fought in the Mexican Wars. For all that they were tough and able to handle themselves in a roughhouse or even shoot a man if need arose, neither Tom, Jack nor Andrew had endured the terrors of battle.

'It's good to have you back again,' said Seth Armstrong, clapping his arm around his young son's shoulders. 'It's been too long. Your ma's been grieving for you.'

'I know,' said Anthony, 'it's a right smart distance from here to Massachusetts, though. I can't be haring back

16

every five minutes.' Then, to change the subject, he said, 'What is it with you and Michael Doolan these days? You still at daggers drawn with each other?'

'You might well say so,' replied his father, rubbing his jaw meditatively. 'Things are no better than when last we saw you and they're like to get a good deal worse.'

'Worse? How so?'

'I don't want to see you mixed up in a lot of dirty business while you're here. Just lend a hand to look after the animals and that'll be all I want of you.'

'Are you in any trouble, Pa?'

'Nothing I can't take care of by my own self, son. I looked after my family these thirty years or more; I reckon I don't need any help.'

Despite this assurance, Anthony was made profoundly uneasy, not especially by his father's words, but more by the old man's attitude. It was plain that something was amiss, but it was equally certain that his father was not about to discuss it.

Since he was a young boy, Anthony had been aware that not all that took place on the Crossed 'A' spread was open and above board. Being the youngest, with a gap of six years between him and his next brother Andrew, Anthony had not been as deep in his father's counsels as the other three boys. Then, when he had shown a brilliant streak for book learning, his father had engaged the minister from Parson's End to give him private lessons in Latin, Greek and other subjects such as were not covered by the syllabus of the town school. The consequence was that it had been studying that his father expected of him as a youth, rather than riding out and dealing with the practical matter of running the place.

'Well, I suppose you know your own business best . . . ' began Anthony, but his father cut in with the greatest irascibility, before he could complete the sentence.

'You talk like a lawyer already and

ain't been studying yet at college above a twelvemonth or so. Lord knows how you'll sound by the time you finish there.'

Feeling that his father might think he was putting on airs and graces, Anthony took breath to deny that he had changed in the least degree since last they had spoken together, before he went off in the fall of 1865. Before he had even formed the words, though, there came the crack of a rifle shot. Seth Armstrong gave a grunt and dropped to the turf.

Unlike his father and brothers, Anthony Armstrong was not in the habit of carrying firearms. It would have looked pretty well out of place on the Harvard campus had he started strolling around with a six-gun tucked in his belt. His father was not moving; just lying still, with his eyes open and staring up at the sky. It wasn't possible to aid him under fire and so the first thing to do was drive off any attacker. He reached down and pulled out the

Navy Colt which hung at his father's hip, cocking it with his thumb as he did so. Then he began scanning the surrounding area, in order to locate the sniper who had taken down his pa.

2

In the May of 1863, Anthony Armstrong had travelled alone from his home in Arizona to Cambridge, Massachusetts in order to take up his place at the Law School at Harvard. He was just eighteen years of age. In the event, he never reached Cambridge. That period was, thought some, a crucial point in the War Between the States, with England supposedly on the verge of recognizing the Confederacy and offering its support to the fledgling nation. Lee, flushed with his victory at Chancellorsville, had just embarked upon the invasion of the North. Anthony, like all his family, hated the very idea of slavery and was hoping to see the South defeated by Mr Lincoln and his army. Whether he was motivated by such noble sentiments as a hatred of the institutions of the South, or perhaps just because he was young and sought adventure, whatever the reason, no sooner had the young boy arrived in Massachusetts than he enlisted in the Federal Army.

From that May of 1863 until the signing of the armistice at Appomattox Court House, two years later, Anthony Armstrong was in the thick of the fiercest fighting ever seen on the North American continent. When his mother got word that he had enlisted in the army, she was struck all of a heap and fainted away dead on the spot. Seth Armstrong was more phlegmatic about it, merely observing that he had done much the same thing himself at a similar age.

There were no furloughs for the Union forces as they fought their way into the southern states and it was two years before Anthony was able to return home to his mother and father. When he fetched up at the farmhouse towards the end of April in 1865, the first person he met was his mother. She gave him such a slap around his face that two of his teeth were loosened. She had never thought to see her beloved baby son again alive.

They all thought that Anthony had ruined his chances of studying at Harvard by vanishing en route in that way, but it appeared not. Indeed, the college expressed their honour at being able to welcome a veteran of the late war into their halls. So it was that after spending the summer of 1865 at home, Anthony Armstrong set off again for Harvard that fall; this time arriving without any detours.

He fitted in well enough at college, but his experiences of war had marked him and everybody knew that he was in some way a man apart. From September 1865 to April 1867, Anthony Armstrong did not leave Massachusetts once and it was only as Easter approached that he felt that it was time to go back to Arizona and see his family again.

Whoever had shot Seth Armstrong

had not stayed around afterwards to see the consequences of it. As Anthony looked round for a target, he heard the drumming of hoof beats on the other side of a rise of ground about a quarter mile from where he lay. At that range, hitting his father could surely have been no more than a fluke. Whoever had fired at them had most likely only intended the shot as a warning and it was mere ill fortune which had led to the ball finding a lodging place in Seth Armstrong's breast.

There was a small, neat hole in his father's shirt, with a little staining around it. Anthony said, 'Pa, can you hear me?'

'Course I can hear you, you young fool,' replied his father quietly. 'You think I been struck deaf? I been shot in the chest, not my ear.'

'Thank the Lord for that,' said his son piously. 'When you didn't move, I thought — '

'Nothin' o' the sort. I don't want to move, not 'til I know where the ball is. I don't want to dislodge it and cause myself a mischief.'

'You want I should look?'

'Course I do, you damn fool. Who else is round to do it?'

Despite his rough words, the old man was right glad that it had been his youngest son near at hand when this misfortune had struck him. Had it been Tom or Jack, they would have gone racing off after the man who had fired the shot, chased the shooter half way across the territory and then killed him. Meanwhile, he himself would have expired quietly, having been quite forgotten in his sons' quest for vengeance. Anthony was a horse of another colour and Seth Armstrong knew that not only would he deal with the wound first before even thinking about any retaliation, but that he probably knew more about tending to bullet wounds than his brothers.

Gingerly, Anthony Armstrong probed the area around the wound in his father's chest. He said, 'Does it hurt when you breathe in, Pa?'

Seth took a deep gulp and said, 'No, not at all. Seems like it ain't through my lung, which is a mercy.'

'Is it painful when I prod you here?'

'Yes, it is, you clumsy oaf. Mind what you're about.'

'You know what I think? I'm thinking that the ball's cracked one of your ribs and now it's just resting in the chest cavity. We can fish it out, and if the wound doesn't turn bad, I think you'll be right as rain.'

His father grunted. 'Ain't you the optimist? Maybe you're right, though. Leastways about the cracked rib. I think the bone took most of the force out o' it and it's just kind of nestled there. Think you can handle it, or need I send to town for the doctor?'

Anthony considered the question seriously for a spell and then said slowly, 'I reckon that doctor or no doctor, I've likely had more experience of this than most men. If you're agreeable, I'll do it for you. It'll hurt like hell, though. And I surely ain't about to do it here, with cowshit all over the place.'

'You think it's nigh enough the surface to fish out?'

'I hope so. But don't you move now. You start walking, you might send it rattling down the Lord knows where. I'll fetch the buckboard and tote you back to the house.'

In front of his father, Anthony had tried to display as much confidence as possible, not wanting his pa to feel anxious, but once he was heading back to the house, his face grew grave. For all that he'd reassured his father, he knew fine well that digging out that ball wasn't apt to be a simple business.

His mother was working in the kitchen and as soon as her son walked through the door, she saw at once that something was amiss. 'Where's your father?'

'Don't worry, there's been an accident.'

'Accident?' said Martha Armstrong

sharply. 'He's taken a fall or what?'

'Not exactly. Listen, I'm going to harness up the buckboard and bring him back here. Can you boil up some water?'

Nothing but her terror at the thought of something bad befalling her husband or sons would have caused Mrs Armstrong to take the Lord's name in vain. She said, 'Mother of God, boy, what ails him?'

'He's been shot,' said her son bluntly. 'I'm going to dig the ball out if I can.'

'Is it mortal? Will he live?'

'I don't know, Ma, and that's the God's honest truth. The sooner I bring him back here, the sooner we'll know.'

His father had not moved at all, having been lying as still and quiet as he could under the circumstances. Anthony said, 'Pa, I'm going to lift you onto the buckboard. Just relax and don't move more than you can help.'

Seth Armstrong said nothing, just nodded. He too knew that there was an excellent chance that the bullet was going to be knocked loose and end up deep in his body. If that happened, he was as good as dead.

The defining feature of Martha Armstrong's life, and also her tragedy, was that none of her daughters had survived infancy. She had lived for over thirty years in an exclusively male environment, which meant that at times such as this, she knew what needed to be done and wasted no time in doing it. She had in the past patched up her husband and sons when they had broken collar bones tumbling from horses, lost teeth in fist fights, needed knife wounds to be sewn up or even the occasional bullet wound to be dressed. This had been her married life, with no leavening of femininity. No comforting of a lovestruck young daughter, no delivering a baby for a daughter; nothing of that sort at all. So it was that when she heard that her husband had been shot, she simply set to and cleared the kitchen, turning it into something resembling a field hospital. The table had been cleared and scrubbed clean; scissors and thread lay at hand, should a wound need stitching.

'Lay him on the table,' Martha told her son, when he appeared, carrying her husband in his arms. When he'd been laid gently down, she went over and said, 'Seth, what's become o' you? You hang on now. Our boy'll do what's needed.' She took her husband's hand and he squeezed it gently, smiling at her.

Meanwhile, Anthony was boiling up a blunt knife and a teaspoon, hoping that they would suffice. While they were in the pot, he went over to his father and unbuttoned his shirt, pulling it back so that the wound was exposed. 'You want some liquor, 'fore we begin? It's going to hurt like the Devil.'

Seth shook his head impatiently, saying, 'Stop fooling round and do it. I stood pain enough before this day.'

After washing his hands and fishing the knife and spoon out of the water, satisfying himself that they were perfectly clean, Anthony started work. His father did not move a muscle while his son inserted the tip of the knife into the wound and jiggled it about a little. He gave a sigh of relief when the knife scraped against something hard and rough. Judging by its position, about an inch or less in, it wasn't a rib. It could only be that he had found the ball. Having satisfied himself that he had found the bullet, he at once withdrew the knife, fearful of pushing the lead ball deeper into the wound. Then, without further hesitation, he picked up the spoon and swiftly gouged it deep into the hole in his father's chest. He aimed well to one side, intending to scoop out a chunk of flesh along with the ball, rather than run the risk of pushing the bullet in further, perhaps out of his reach.

Throughout the whole of this sickeningly painful procedure, his father stayed completely still and made no sound at all. When he had finished, though, Anthony noticed beads of bright blood on his father's lower lip where he had bitten it. The ball came out in the spoon, dropping to the floor as he yanked it out. He said to his mother, 'We'd best dress that wound. It won't do to leave it open to the air like that.'

'I'll do it. I hear horses outside. You'd better see who it is.'

A sudden apprehension of danger gripped him and Anthony strode over to the wall and took down the scattergun which was hanging there. He cocked both hammers and then went to the door, kicking it open and marching straight out into the yard with the gun held to his shoulder.

Tom, Jack and Andrew were more than a little taken aback to find their baby brother drawing down on them with a shotgun. Tom said, 'What in the hell are you playing at, little brother? What's goin' on?'

'Pa's been shot. Thought you three might have come to finish off the job.'

'Shot?' exclaimed Tom. 'Who shot him? Is he all right?'

'I've just taken the ball out. I think he'll do. As for who shot him, I was hoping you boys could tell me that.'

The three men on horseback looked sideways at each other, none of them wishing to be the one to explain. At length, Tom said, 'Pa doesn't want you getting mixed up in anything. He's that proud o' you, you goin' to be a lawyer and all. Said as he'd skin any one of us as told you any of our games.'

'This something to do with the Doolans?'

'You might say so,' said Jack.

'Ma know what it's about?'

'She guesses plenty, but you know her. She never asks nothing.'

Anthony lowered the scattergun and carefully uncocked the piece. Then he said, 'We'll talk on this later. For now, we all know that somebody tried to kill Pa. We'd best set a guard on the house. I'm not fixing for any harm to come to either Ma or Pa.'

The four of them entered the kitchen, to find their mother winding a bandage around her husband's chest. She turned round from this task and said abruptly, 'I don't want you boys milling round and causing a fuss. Stay out now, 'til I got your pa comfortable.'

This was pretty plain talking and so the young men backed out of the kitchen and strolled together in the general direction of the barn. Anthony said, 'By the by, I noticed Pa's not as sharp as he once was. Any of you seen that too?'

'That's the nub o' the matter, in a manner of speaking,' said Tom slowly, 'meaning that Pa ain't exactly his self lately. He's forgetful, don't know half the time what we're up to.'

Jack chimed in, saying, 'So's not to shame him, we don't say over much 'bout it. Like it might be he says, 'You boys get on with what needs doing,' but then later on he's cursin' up hill and down dale on account of he's forgot where we are.'

Anthony frowned. 'That happen often?'

'Most days lately,' said Andrew, 'an' it's gettin' worse. He gets confused too about things. Couple o' days back, he was talkin' 'bout you coming home and said as you'd been in the army a fair spell. He'd forgot about Harvard an' all, thought you was still at war.'

'What does Ma say?' asked Anthony, 'She know all this?'

'Sure she does,' said Tom, 'but she won't talk to us about it none. Don't want to think on it, I guess.'

The four of them stopped by the barn and his brothers lit up and stood smoking for a space. Then Anthony asked, 'So who shot him? Don't say you don't know, 'cause I can tell you weren't surprised to hear it. What's going on?'

None of his three brothers spoke for a while and it was fairly clear to Anthony that there were things going on from which they hoped to shield him. How much of this was because he was their baby brother and to what extent it was that his pa had never wanted to see him involved in dishonest business he could not say. But he was determined to find out what the score was, so that he could help to protect his father.

At last, Tom said, 'Here's the way of it. You know how Pa was always willin' to deal in steers which weren't always bought straight and paid for?'

'Knew stuff like that was done,' said Anthony, 'I never needed any of you to tell me about it. I have eyes in my head.'

'Well then,' continued Tom, 'lately, cattle has been a drag on the market. Price has dropped 'til it ain't hardly worth takin' 'em to sell. Something to do with railheads being set up in Kansas and herds drove up from Texas. Whatever 'tis, it's been the ruination of us and the Doolans both.'

Anthony cast his gaze around the house and barn and the rolling land around them, which stretched as far as the eye could see for hundreds of acres. He said, 'We don't look to be paupers yet awhile.'

'Well, it ain't from steers. It's horses.'

'You're breeding horses? Or buying and selling them? I never knew that. When did that all start?'

'We ain't breedin' of 'em, nor buyin' 'em neither,' said Jack, staring moodily towards the distant horizon. 'We're stealin' 'em.'

'You're stealing horses?' exclaimed Anthony, aghast. 'Landsakes, what's the matter with you all? Is this Pa's idea?'

'What it is, Anthony,' said Andrew, 'is that Pa was always right good at knowing about how to deal in steers. When the bottom fell out o' that market, he was lost. Couldn't cope or think what to do next. Me and the others, we kind of stepped in and branched out, as you might say.'

'Horses, though!' said Anthony, genuinely shocked.

In Washington or New York, the theft of a horse was no great matter. You might fetch up in the courthouse for taking a man's horse, but you'd be unlucky to get more than a fine for it. Out in the western territories, though, things were very different. The theft of a horse could condemn a man to a lingering death in the desert or leave him at the mercy of bloodthirsty savages. Horses had an almost mystical significance for those living in wild country on the edge of the frontier. Few types were more despised than horse thieves and the fellow who ventured into that line of work was just begging to end up being invited to a necktie party and jerked to Jesus at the end of a hang-rope.

'Pa thinks that we're still taking mavericks and such and raisin' them ourselves,' said Jack. 'He's afeared that you'll hear of it and he wants you to stay out of trouble, seein' as you're set to be a lawyer. He don't know nothin' about the horses, though. Not a damn thing. You're not to say a word to him about all this, neither.'

Anthony's mind had been working rapidly and he thought that he knew now what had precipitated the attempt on his father's life. He said, 'I'm guessing then that the Doolans have their tails in the same crack and you're all competing for the same goods. Is that the strength of it?'

'Pretty much,' Tom said. 'Old man Doolan's been hiring more men lately and we've been expectin' something. Not this, though.'

'I'll ride over to see him tonight,' said Anthony, 'see if I can make the peace with him. This can't carry on, not with Pa wounded and Ma there in the house.'

'You can't go up to Doolan's by yourself,' Tom told him flatly. 'If it's got as far as shooting, then they'll think nothing of shooting you down as well.'

'I don't think so. I always got on well enough with Mr Doolan and his boys. Anyways, he knows I'm nothing to do with all this, having been out East for all that time. I'll reason with him. You'll see, it'll be fine.'

Jack interrupted at this point, saying to his brothers, 'Anthony's got a point. He don't carry iron and see how he's dressed. They won't trouble him and Mr Doolan always had a soft spot for him, 'fore him and Pa fell out.'

When they went back into the house, it was to find that their father had been helped to bed by his wife and was resting. She'd examined the wound and splashed some lye round it. From all that she could see it was clean enough and with a little luck, her husband would pull through. When her four sons were settled in the kitchen, Martha said to them, 'I don't inquire as to what's going on, but I tell you now I don't want any one of you seeking vengeance or any foolishness of that kind. I look to you, Tom, to put a stop to this and I don't mean by going off and shooting Michael Doolan, either. You hear what I tell you?'

'Sure, Ma,' said Tom. 'Anthony says he's a goin' to ride there and smooth things over with 'em. Try to make peace.'

His mother looked long and searchingly at Anthony and then nodded her head slowly. 'I'll allow there's some sense in that scheme. The boy's got a head on his shoulders and what's more he uses it, which is more than can be said for some folk as I could mention.' She said to Anthony, 'When you going over there, son?'

'I thought in an hour or two. Nobody has any objection, I'll take the bay mare.'

'Mind yourself. There's some rare scoundrels hunkered down round the Doolan spread these days. Ragamuffins and scamps from both armies, men as have nothing to do but fight and suchlike. You mind how you step.'

Anthony looked back steadily at his mother and said quietly, 'It's like I told the others, Ma. I'll reason with them.'

3

It had been some four or five years since he had been on the Doolan spread and Anthony Armstrong looked about him with great interest. After his brothers had told him about the problems with cattle, it had drawn his attention to the fact that there were fewer steers around than had been the case before he went off to war. Now, riding across the Doolans' land, he could see the same thing. Few cattle, but few horses too. He hadn't asked his brothers where they were keeping the horses that they were taking. He would have to look into that when he got home.

The Doolans' house was not as well appointed or large as that in which the Armstrongs lived, but it was substantial enough. When Anthony rode into the yard surrounding the house, there was no sign of either Michael Doolan or his sons, Ezra and Joe. There was a small knot of men branding a horse in a corral which ran alongside the barn. When they became aware of his presence, they stopped what they were doing and two of them walked over, presumably to ask him his business. Anthony half expected to see the fellow Hogan, who he had knocked down in the street in Parson's End, but found that neither of the men who came to talk to him were Hogan.

'You a preacher or somethin'?' was the first question addressed to him. Anthony, recollecting that the purpose of his mission was a pacific one, did not rise to the bait, but instead paused a second or two before replying.

'I'm no preacher. Why would you think so?'

'You sure dress like a minister. Well, what're you after?'

'I'm looking to speak to Michael Doolan. He knows me well enough. Is he about?'

On learning that this sober and well-spoken stranger was apparently an acquaintance of their boss, the man to whom Anthony was speaking grew a little more polite. He said, 'The boss went over to Parson's End on business. We don't rightly know when he'll be back.'

'What about Joe or Ezra? Are they anywhere to be found?'

'They're away as well.'

Had the matter been less urgent, then the young man would most probably have ridden off and returned at a later date, but this was life and death. There had been one shooting; he had to make sure that there wasn't another. That being so, he dismounted and said pleasantly, 'I reckon I'll just wait until one of them shows up, in that case.'

A look of alarm came into the faces of the two men standing on the other side of the fence surrounding the corral. The one to whom he had been speaking said, 'Hey, you can't do that!'

'Can I not? I'm paying a friendly visit to a neighbour. Who are you to say who can come and visit Mr Doolan?'

As he watched their faces, Anthony saw comprehension slowly flooding into their brains. 'Neighbour? Where you from?'

'My name's Anthony Armstrong and I live over yonder.' He waved in the direction of his home. 'I've been away for a spell and now I'm back; I'm making a few visits.'

The other three men who had been clustered around the horse they were branding, had also stopped work and were standing watching him. It took no great art to read their minds and figure out what was going through them. First off was that these men probably knew about the shooting at him and his father. It could even be that one of them had actually pulled the trigger. Second, that horse that they were branding was stolen, for a bet, which was making them nervous. Then again, they could see that Anthony wasn't carrying a gun, which meant that there was no question of goading him into a duel so that they could be rid of him that way. Lastly, of course, they didn't wish to take upon themselves the responsibility for killing or even provoking a fight with somebody, right on their boss's doorstep, until they had direct instructions. Old Mr Doolan was the very Devil when he was roused.

Notwithstanding their doubts, the five men in the corral were moving forward in a way that suggested that they might start something anyway, simply because they didn't have the sense to deal with an unaccustomed situation without resorting to violence. Anthony was preparing himself mentally for a fight and was wondering if it would be limited to fists and boots or if one of these men would try to kill him with a knife, when there came a shout from the direction of the big house. It was a woman's voice and she called, 'Anthony Armstrong, ain't you going to come and greet me? It's been a good long while since you came by here.'

He turned and saw that Mr Doolan's wife Susan was hurrying towards him, a broad smile of greeting upon her plump and good-natured face. She gave a baleful look at the five men who were moving in on Anthony and said, 'You scallywags get on with your work now. And if you see Mr Armstrong here coming to visit, you best be as polite as you know how, or you'll have me to answer to!' With that, she turned and led Anthony into the house.

When she had seated him comfortably in the kitchen and set a pot of coffee on the stove to boil, Mrs Doolan said, 'It must be four years now since we've seen you here. Too long.'

It was difficult to know how to respond to such an opening, because Anthony guessed that Michael Doolan's wife would naturally take her husband's side in any dispute between the two families. The stout woman fussing about at the range must have read his mind, for she said, 'Oh, I know that your pa and my Mick, Mr Doolan I should say, have their differences, but you and Ezra were always good friends and it grieved me to see us be sundered like that. Why, Martha, your ma that is, and me, time was when we was like sisters. In and out of each other's company every chance we had.'

'To tell you the truth, ma'am,' said Anthony slowly and with an embarrassed air, 'I don't even know what happened to end our friendship. Only that Pa and Mr Doolan had some species of falling out.'

'It was something and nothing. Your pa reckoned as Mr Doolan had registered a brand without telling him. You know they were more or less partners at one time. One thing led to another, there was high words and the upshot was that the two of 'em stopped speaking. And then Mick, Mr Doolan, told me and the boys to give you all a wide berth into the bargain.'

'Pretty much the self-same thing happened at our house.'

'Well, it was no affair of yours, at any rate. It's good to see you setting there. How is your ma? I see her odd times in town, but we don't generally speak. Just kind o' nod at each other, like we was practically strangers.'

'She's fine,' said Anthony, 'much the same as usual.'

'She as tough on you boys as ever?'

Recollecting how she had swiped Jack around the head with the soup ladle, Anthony had to smother a grin. 'She's still tough enough, ma'am, yes.'

Seeing the laughter that the youngster was suppressing, gave Susan Doolan to hope that she could share with him a story that had gone round Parson's End the previous fall. She said, 'I suppose you mightn't have heard how she went for your brother Jack this winter gone?'

'Went for him? How so?'

'This'd be maybe three or four months back. Jack was supposed to be doing something or other, I don't mind what, but your ma she couldn't find

49

him nohow. Somehow, she found out as he was at play in the Lucky Lady. Believe it or believe it not, Martha, she walked five miles to town, a-carrying with her a hickory stick. Well Jack, he's at the gaming table and playing cards for high stakes, when in walks your ma. She marches straight up to where those boys are playing and she lands that hickory stick 'cross Jack's shoulders. The dealer, he says to Martha, 'What are you about, you old hagling? We's playing poker here; this ain't a fit place for women to be.' Your ma, she didn't say nothing at all to that man, but she ups and whacks him round the head with the hickory stick and would you believe it, lays him out stone cold. Then she grabs your brother by the ear and marches him out the saloon, with him saying, 'Ma, you're shaming me!' '

So ridiculous was the story and so exactly like his mother, that Anthony threw back his head and let out a bellow of laughter. Then, wondering if he wasn't in some way being disloyal to his family, he tried to make his face straight again.

Mrs Doolan said, 'Mind, I don't think that Jack was shamed in any way. I doubt there was a man in the territories that durst have interfered with your ma that night, not with her on the rampage and brandishing that hickory stick.'

It was as plain as day to Anthony Armstrong that after sitting like this and laughing with Susan Doolan, he couldn't have any sort of showdown with her husband that evening. He said, 'Well, it's sure been good to visit with you again, ma'am. I'm sorry things have turned out as they have. You might tell Mr Doolan that I came here because I'm hopeful of making the peace between him and my pa.'

'I'll be sure to tell him, son.'

'Katy and Maire not around, I suppose?' asked Anthony, a little wistfully.

'They gone into town with they brothers.'

'Well, be sure to tell them that I said 'hallo'. You might say to your husband that I want to avoid any further trouble between us and that my pa is still in the land of the living yet.'

Mrs Doolan cocked her head to one side, saying, 'What's this? Why shouldn't your pa be in the land of the living? What ain't you told me?'

'Ma'am, maybe your husband didn't know about it, but somebody shot my pa this day. He's lying abed at our house this very minute.'

Her hand went to her mouth and the colour blanched from her face. Susan Doolan said, 'Lord a mercy, you don't say so. Tell me this is naught of my husband's doing?'

'I don't know whose doing it is, Mrs Doolan, but I'm afeared as there'll be murder done if we don't stop this feud right this minute. Please tell your husband I came by to see him and that I meant well by him.'

⋆ ⋆ ⋆

What might have been an amusing story for the folks in and around Parson's End was anything but likely to raise a smile from Jack Armstrong. He still burned with humiliation every time he recollected that fearful scene in the saloon, with his mother marching him out of the place like an errant schoolboy; and him twenty-eight years of age.

He had always had a partiality and weakness for intoxicating liquor, but since that frightful incident, just before the Christmas of 1866, Jack had taken to drinking alone, which is generally a bad sign in a man of any age, but is liable to lead to particular mischief in a younger person. Although it was in general seen as a fine, manly quality to possess, it was Jack's ability to 'hold his liquor' as the saying goes that provided the spark which set the powder train burning that week.

If, after getting liquored up, Jack Armstrong had been the kind of fellow to reel all over the shop, so that everybody could see he was drunk as a fiddler's bitch, then more note might have been taken of the heavy drinking habit into which he had slipped between Christmas and Easter. As it was, his trips to the barn, where he kept a flagon of poteen, passed unremarked and he was frequently the worse for wear by the time he came to his bed.

That evening, on the day that his younger brother had returned from college, Jack was seething with fury. Although he loved Anthony dearly, it had always seemed to him that both his mother and father favoured their youngest son over him, Tom and Andrew. Who in the hell did Anthony think he was, riding off like that to the Doolans' to act as peacemaker? That role should surely have fallen to either Jack or Tom, the two eldest brothers.

Then there was the shooting of his father. Although it looked like his pa would live, it was not to be thought of that those responsible for this cowardly attempt at assassination should escape quite unscathed. At the very least, they should be warned off and given to understand that any further action of that sort would bring down lightning upon their heads. Peacemaking? What those skunks needed was a good scare to put the fear of God into them and ensure that they would not essay any scurvy tricks of that sort in the future.

When Anthony returned from the Doolans', he gave out that there was not likely to be any further attack on them or their property and told them the gist of his conversation with Mrs Doolan. Once again, that cursed story made even his own brothers chuckle. Well, if there were really people living thereabouts who thought that Jack Armstrong was a figure of fun, then they were in for an almighty shock before the night was out, that was all. He would show everybody, once for all, that he was not a man to be taken lightly.

It was getting on for midnight when

Jack saddled up and rode north. In a pack affixed to the back of the saddle were some long branches with cotton wound round the ends and tacked on tight, a can of lamp oil and three empty hessian sugar sacks with two holes cut in each. In addition to this material, there was a carbine held in a scabbard at front of the saddle; Jack also had his pistol slapping against his thigh.

Three miles north of the Armstrong house were thirty acres of land farmed, after a fashion, by a man called Jed Stone. Stone's farming activities were by way of being a sideline, some said a blind, for his real business. This consisted in part of moonshining and running guns to the Indians, and also acting as custodian of the horses that the Armstrong brothers acquired from various sources. Stone and the man he shared his cabin with were required to do nothing more taxing than keep the livestock that Jack, Tom and Andrew brought to their land penned up in a little blind gulley on their land for a week or two at a time, making sure that they were watered and fed. There was a considerable risk involved in this, for if Jed and his friend Albert Donague were found in possession of the animals by their owners, they would most likely be strung up on the spot. He was accordingly well paid for his services. It was Jed Stone's home that Jack was riding for that night.

Fortunately, there was a full moon, which reduced the chances of Jack's horse putting her foot in a hole and breaking a leg. She was an intelligent beast and her native caution made up a little for the slightly befuddled state of the man riding her. At any rate, she contrived to get her owner safely to Jed and Albert's cabin. As Jack reined in, Jed emerged, having heard the hoof beats. 'Oh, it's you!' he said with a distinct lack of enthusiasm. Of the three brothers with whom he dealt, Jed Stone found Jack the least pleasant company.

'I want some help from you fellows,' said Jack, with no preamble. 'Got a little job wants doing.'

'At this time o' night? Can't it wait 'til mornin'?'

'Listen, Stone, you want to keep taking our cash for just keeping a few horses out here, you best lend a hand this night. Else we and you are like to part company, you get what I'm a-saying?'

Two things were crystal clear to Jed Stone. The first was that Jack had been drinking and was in an ugly mood. Second was where the man was quite capable, if irritated, of terminating the business arrangement the Armstrongs had with Jed and Albert. This would be the deuce of a nuisance and so Jed found it politic to invite the other into his home to talk over what he had in mind.

Once Jack was comfortably ensconced in the log cabin which Jed and Albert called home, he outlined his plan and from the first, both Jed Stone and Albert had a premonition of disaster. There seemed little possibility of talking Jack out of his mad plan, though, and so, rather than risk losing their income from the Armstrongs, they agreed to go along with what was suggested.

'I had about enough of those Doolans,' announced Jack, when he had been furnished with a glass of the latest batch of poteen distilled by Jed. 'Tonight's the night that we put a scare into 'em.'

'How so?' asked Jed.

'Out on the back of my saddle, I got some stuff. Wait up while I fetch it in.' Jack went out to his horse, giving Albert and Jed the opportunity to exchange glances and roll their eyes meaningfully. When he returned to the cabin, Jack showed them what he was carrying. First, he handed them the hessian bags with holes cut in them. They looked at these in frank bewilderment.

'What are these for?' asked Albert.

'What are they for? Why, you chucklehead, they're masks. Spook masks.'

'For why? What're we like to need them for?'

'The Doolan boys have gone off for a few days. It'll just be Mick and his wife, alone in the house. We're going to give 'em a fright is all. See here, I got torches as well. We're going to ride up to the house and just set on our horses in front. Then we'll fire in the air a couple o' times, kind of let 'em know we're there. We won't say nothing, just sit there holding our torches and them not able to see our faces. Then we ride out.'

Neither Albert nor Jed could see any sense at all in the projected enterprise, but nor could they see that it would do much harm. If this was to be the limit of what Jack wanted of them and if it would keep him sweet, then it was worth the trouble. Jed said, 'You take oath as there's no more to the matter than that? We're just going to fire in the air and sit outside they house, looking menacing. You ain't a fixin' for to kill any of them or nothin' of that sort?'

'I give you both my word,' said Jack solemnly, 'I just want to warn 'em to stay clear of us in the future. Even without they see our faces, they'll know what it's all about. I'll warrant they'll take the message sure enough.'

4

Whether you are running a rolling mill in Pittsburgh or dealing in horseflesh out in some western territory, the same iron laws of economics will apply to your business transactions. Among these inflexible principles, as fixed and immutable as the laws of the Medes and Persians, were two which applied especially to the Armstrong and Doolan families at that time and lay at the root of the troubles which were about to engulf them. First, demand stimulates supply. Secondly, competition tends inexorably to force down profits.

When the cattle market in the southern states and territories ceased to become profitable, Michael Doolan had seen that horses were, at least for the time being, likely to be a better bet for trading. Seth Armstrong's boys came to a similar conclusion at about the same time. By then, the two families were no longer on speaking terms and so were in rivalry from the very beginning of their forays into horse trading. Both families soon found that buying and selling horses was unlikely to restore their fortunes and so swiftly turned to acquiring their stock through other means. At first, they went on the scout, picking up whatever they could, but it soon became apparent that they would only be getting two or three beasts at a time by this method — not to mention where the risks of being shot at or caught and lynched were uncomfortably high. All of which led to both families, each unknown to the other, making arrangements with the nearby Zuni Indians and enlisting their aid.

The Zuni hated the white men living in the northern part of New Mexico and Arizona and were happy to raid homesteads and even small towns, riding off with as many horses as they could manage. These they sold to the Doolans and Armstrongs. They had no more love for the two families than they did for any other white men and soon saw that there was opportunity to rack up the price on the stolen animals they sold. They told the Armstrongs that if they wouldn't pay what was asked, then the Doolans would. The same line worked with the Doolans and so by the spring of 1867, even dealing wholesale in stolen horses was not sufficient to maintain the rival families as their sole source of income.

Jack Armstrong's information was slightly out, because one of Michael Doolan's sons had returned home that evening. When Jack, Jed and Albert splashed lamp oil over their torches and lit them at about one in the morning, the Doolans' house contained, in addition to Michael and his wife, their son Ezra and their two daughters, namely Katy and Maire.

The first that Michael Doolan knew of any danger that night was when he was awoken by two pistol shots fired right beneath his bedroom window. He was awake and conscious at once and immediately aware of the flickering light of flames, which he could see dancing on the ceiling above him. Fearing that somebody had torched the barn or, God forbid, the house itself, Doolan leaped from his bed and went racing downstairs. He was in such a state that he didn't even stop to pick up the gun which hung at the foot of his bed. His wife had also been woken by the shooting and chased after her husband in an ecstasy of terror for what might befall him.

Not hesitating for the merest fraction of a second, Doolan opened the front door and ran into the yard, wearing only his nightshirt. He was confronted by three riders holding flaming torches. The faces of all three of the men were obscured by spook masks and two of them were holding their torches in their left hands and clutching pistols in the other. He might have been sixty-one years of age, but nothing daunted Doolan when he was acting in defence of his own family. He roared, 'What the hell are you men about?'

There came no reply from any of the men. Doolan's wife had also come out of the house and was approaching him from behind. Doolan said, 'Get back in the house, Sue. I'll deal with these scamps.'

Susan Doolan ignored this command and went up to her husband, placing her hand on his arm beseechingly, saying, 'Lord, come away out of this, Mick. You ain't even carrying your gun.'

Even now, things might well have passed without any bloodshed if Ezra Doolan, who had also been roused by the gunfire, had not rattled up the casement window of his own bedroom and poked out a sawn-off scattergun that he always kept handy by his bed. He called down at the riders, 'You boys throw down your weapons, or I'll kill every man-jack o' you!'

Then three things happened in quick succession. Susan Doolan clutched her husband and yelled up at her impetuous son, 'Ezra, don't do it, son!' At almost the same instant, Ezra Doolan, fearing that his parents were about to be massacred, let fly with the scattergun hitting Jed Stone in his side. The third thing to occur was that Jack Armstrong, three parts drunk, tightened his grip automatically on the pistol he held when he heard the boom of the shotgun. His piece was cocked and went off at once. The ball took Susan Doolan in the face and she fell back at once, mortally wounded.

Realizing that their plans had miscarried, the three men on horseback whirled round and rode off into the night, casting away their torches as they went.

Outside the Doolans' house, the old man was kneeling beside the lifeless body of his wife, sobbing like a little child and talking frantically to her, as if by so doing he could ward off the reality that she was dead. He said in a low voice, 'Come on, my love, it'll be all right, you'll see. Rouse up, things will be fine. Sue, come now.' His son and daughters had come down the stairs and stood there watching the heart-rending scene; not one of them had the least notion how to deal with such an unexpected situation. None of them had ever seen their father cry or even display much emotion before and the sight was a disturbing one.

Next morning at breakfast, Andrew and Tom noticed that Jack was absent and that his bed did not appear to have been slept in. Their mother said uneasily, 'I hope this has naught to do with your pa's mishap yesterday.' Only Martha Armstrong would have referred to a failed assassination as a 'mishap'.

'I don't believe it's that, Ma,' said Anthony, 'I'm telling you, Mrs Doolan seemed not to know anything about the business. I don't think for a minute that either Mr Doolan or his sons had any part in this.'

'Well then,' said Tom, a little nettled at how much his younger brother appeared to be taking upon himself, 'where do you say Jack might be?'

'I couldn't say,' replied Anthony, 'drunk, maybe?'

'Drunk?' exclaimed Andrew disbelievingly, 'why I never saw the like o' Jack at holding his liquor. I never seed him set drunk since he was a boy.'

Anthony shrugged. He had his own views on the matter and suspected that Jack would be sleeping in some out of the way place, rather than having been shot down by an ambush-killer.

While they were drinking their coffee, Jack turned up. He had, as Anthony had already guessed, spent the night in the barn, sleeping off the ill-effects of his overindulgence. 'You look like hell, man!' was Tom's greeting, followed almost at once by an apology to his mother, who had turned round, ready to take a tough stance were she to hear any more strong language.

'You talk too much,' was all that Jack had to say. 'Any o' that coffee left?'

It was abundantly clear that something was up, but none of Jack's brothers felt inclined to push him on the subject; they figured that he would tell them what was going on in his own good time. Not so Martha Armstrong, who said, 'I was worried. What ails you, son?'

'It's nothing, Ma. I'm fine.'

'I know that look of yours, Jack Armstrong,' his mother said firmly. 'It's the self-same look you had when you were a little boy and had been at the cookie jar. Now what's to do? You know I'll have it out of you, so you might as well tell me now.'

'How's Pa?' asked Jack, still prevaricating.

'He'll do well enough,' replied his mother, 'now what scrape've you been in now?'

Jack sat there for a spell, supping his coffee, before saying, 'I went by the Doolan place last night. Me and a couple o' others. There was shooting.'

There was consternation and Jack's brothers all began asking him questions at once. Their mother banged a pot lid on the stove to quell the hubbub and then spoke. 'Anybody hurt? Killed?'

'One of the boys I was riding with caught a load of buckshot, but we picked it out after we left.' His mother's eye was still fixed upon him and so slowly and unwillingly, Jack continued, 'I think I might o' shot somebody as well.'

It took a while to extract a full and complete account of the episode from Jack and when they had done so, his mother said, 'Not a word of this to your pa. I don't want him frettin'. You boys had best make sure that you set a watch for trouble. If Michael Doolan's still living, he'll be on the vengeance trail for this piece of work. If it was Susan . . . '

Something which all four of the brothers marked was that their ma wasted no time in recriminations or anything of the sort. For her, the case was clearcut. One of her boys was in trouble and she would stand up for him come hell or high water. She expected no less of the rest of them. This was one of those occasions when they would all have to pull together. There would be time later to castigate her son for his folly, but that time most decidedly was not now. She walked over to Jack and laid her hand on his shoulder. He looked up at his mother and she said, 'What we goin' to do with you, boy? You always been a torment to me.' She smiled as she spoke these harsh words, which took the sting from them. Then she said in a louder voice, 'You boys better be ready for trouble. Your pa ain't fit to handle it, so it falls to the four of you.'

Tom cleared his throat and said hesitantly, 'Pa said as we wasn't to mix Anthony up in any of our business. He was most particular 'bout it.'

Martha Armstrong said softly, 'Anthony's one of the family, same as you boys. He'll do what's necessary. Don't you worry about what Pa says for now. Just recollect that I still have my stick near at hand and be sure to do what I say. Now get along with you all, I have to tend to Pa.'

When Susan Doolan had taxed her

husband the previous evening with ordering, or being concerned in, or having any part in the shooting of Seth Armstrong, he had been genuinely perplexed. He and his former partner might be at outs and not on good terms, but the idea that he would try to kill his former friend was a strange one. His wife could see at once that he was telling the truth and so the matter was left there. When the Doolans had retired that night it had been agreed that Michael Doolan would, notwithstanding the tension between the families, ride over to the Armstrong house the following day and offer his sympathy. He also determined to find out if any of his men might have had a hand in the affair.

Tim Hogan had been mightily ticked off to be knocked down in the street by a sawn-off runt dressed like a Sunday school superintendent. On the way back to the Doolan place, Mr Doolan happened to mention that the young man who had assaulted him was one of the Armstrong brothers. After getting back to the big house, Hogan and his partner Trent Barker went out to collect a couple of horses which were waiting for them on the other side of the river. Barker told the men they collected the horses from all about how Hogan had been beaten up by a fellow half his size. They found this funny and began twitting him about it, whereupon he lost his patience, which of course provoked even more amusement.

It should be said that Hogan was a man who took himself very seriously and if there was one thing in this world that he could not stomach, it was folk making a game of him. On the way back with the horses, Hogan told Barker in no uncertain terms to watch his step and then he dug his spurs viciously in his own mount's flanks and headed over the hill in the direction of the Armstrongs' place.

As he approached the rise of ground that separated the fields lying alongside the river from the corrals and buildings of the Armstrong house, Hogan dismounted and pulled the rifle from the scabbard at front of his saddle and then walked slowly up the incline. It was a thousand to one against seeing the fellow who had humiliated him, but it was surely worth a look. He could scarcely believe his luck when he came to the crest of the little hill and saw both the man who had knocked him down and also the man whose actions were always frustrating the profits of the family for whom he worked.

Seth Armstrong and his little son, who had, according to Mr Doolan, been away at college, were just standing there, chatting. The fury which had been simmering away in Hogan's breast came welling up at the sight of the man who had attacked him and he knelt down and raised his rifle. You could say many harsh and unpleasant things about Tim Hogan, but you would have to concede that he was a superb shot. Had it not been for the slight gust of wind which blew just as he squeezed the trigger, there could be no doubt that Anthony Armstrong would have dropped dead on the spot. At getting on for five hundred yards, though, the distance Hogan was from his target, that little puff of spring air was all that was needed to cause his ball to veer off by a foot or so, burying itself instead in the chest of the elder Mr Armstrong.

Firing a shot at the man who had knocked him into the dust back at Parson's End acted as a catharsis on Hogan and although he saw immediately that he had hit the father, rather than the son, the fact that he had shot somebody assuaged his feelings. He threw himself to the turf and wriggled back the way he had come, taking great care not to show himself above the skyline as he would be seen from down below. Then he jumped on his horse and headed back to the Doolan spread, his good humour entirely restored.

So it was that the man who was ultimately to blame for the tragic events which befell not only the Armstrong and Doolan families, but also various other people, that man had been motivated by nothing more important than a temporary loss of face outside a barroom.

While the Armstrong brothers were preparing to defend themselves against the attack which they felt would not be long in coming after Jack's foolish adventure the previous night, Michael Doolan was laying out his wife of thirty-eight years. His daughters, grief-stricken as they were, offered to undertake the job, but Doolan would hear nothing of the sort. He turfed them all out of the large room at the front of the house and laid Sue's body upon the mahogany dining table. The bullet had wrought havoc with her face, which was in consequence a hideous sight to behold. After fetching a basin and mopping away the congealed blood and fragments of white bone where her cheekbone had been shattered, he sponged down her hair, trying to make it as soft as it had been in life.

When he had finished cleaning up the wreckage of his poor dead wife's face, Michael Doolan went upstairs to choose an outfit for her. He couldn't bear to think of her being buried in her nightgown, looking so homely and mundane. The best dress Susan owned was the one she wore on her infrequent visits to church. This he carried down to where his wife was lying. From the kitchen came the sound of sobbing. His daughters were taking it hard and Doolan knew that he would have to send them away for a while, until he had cleared everything up and settled matters to his own satisfaction.

He had no idea about undergarments and the like, but he figured that Sue would understand that and not hold it against him. He eased the nightgown over her head, the rigour having left her by now. Then he carefully lifted her arms and somehow manoeuvred her into the dress. It was enough for now and Doolan knew that if he continued much longer at the task, he would break down in tears again. That was the last thing he needed to be doing at this time. All else apart, the girls needed his strength. Moreover, Ezra and Joe would have to be instructed in the steps necessary to be revenged upon the cowards who had gunned down their mother.

When he entered the kitchen, the girls were seated at the table, weeping, just as he had suspected would be the case. Ezra was standing by the window. From the redness in the boy's eyes, Doolan guessed that he too had shed tears that morning. Well, there was no shame in that. He said, 'Katy, why don't you and your sister start thinking about getting yourselves washed and tidied up. We can't be mourning all the day long. Go along now.'

The brisk manner that Doolan adopted with the girls acted on them like a tonic and they obediently stood up, preparatory to going up the stairs and making themselves ready to face the coming day. As they left, they both stopped to kiss their father on the cheek. When they had left the room, Doolan went over and quietly closed the door, so that he and his son would not be overheard.

'Where's that brother of your'n?' he asked of his son.

'He said as he'd be back today, Pa. You want I should go hunt for him?'

'No, that ain't needed. We can start layin' our plans before he gets here.'

'Plans? You mean the . . . the funeral and such?'

'That too,' said Doolan, 'yes, one of us'll have to ride into town and talk to the minister. But that weren't what I had in mind.'

'What then?' asked Ezra.

'Why, boy, I needs must spell it out? You value your ma's life so cheap as you'd let those mangy dogs that gunned her down go free?'

★ ★ ★

Sheriff Brewster Bates had nominal responsibility for maintaining law and order in Parson's End, but it was not by way of being an especially arduous job. Bates collected local taxes, and made sure that drunkenness was discouraged and that new buildings were not erected willy nilly all over the place. There was little crime in the town and what there was was, as a rule, settled by personal means, rather than by telling tales to the law. Sheriff Bates turned a blind eye to many things, but as the town seemed to prosper under this benign neglect, nobody was much bothered. Brewster Bates had been voted in for the last five years, largely on account of nobody else felt inclined to take on the role of sheriff. He was a good-natured and idle man, who had turned fifty that year. His only aim in life was to continue in his present post until he was too old to be able to walk or see.

Just lately, there had been a fly in the ointment of Sheriff Bates' previously tranquil professional existence. This had been the alarming increase in raids by the Zuni and Navaho Indians. Some people had been killed, but the main thing was the loss of livestock — principally horses. It was rumoured that if things got any worse, then the army might send a unit to the area to suppress such lawlessness. This was a development that Bates was excessively anxious to avoid at all costs. Brewster Bates was nobody's fool and he had, almost from the moment that he took up his post, been taking money from both the Armstrongs and the Doolans. He had understood that this was to ensure that he turned a blind eye to the altering of brands and suchlike. Lately, though, since the virtual collapse of the cattle trade in this part of the country, Bates had an uncomfortable feeling that both Seth Armstrong and Mick Doolan were up to other things.

The day after Anthony Armstrong arrived in Parson's End, Brewster Bates was sitting in his office, re-reading a letter which had come in on the mail coach the previous day. It was ten in the morning and too early for fretting about such things, but Bates knew that he was soon going to be compelled to have a serious word with both the Armstrongs and the Doolans and tell them to scale back their activities, at least for a while. The letter in his hand was from the commander of a fort in New Mexico; copies had apparently been sent to all law enforcement officers in the northern parts of Arizona and New Mexico. The gist of it was that unless the civilian sheriffs and marshals could keep a lid on the depredations which were now becoming widespread, then a cavalry column would soon be conducting a sweep of the area. This was far from being an attractive prospect. Nobody wanted a bunch of damned soldiers poking their snouts into everybody's business.

It was while Sheriff Brewster was engrossed in this missive, that the door opened and in walked two grim-faced men. He recognized immediately Mick

Doolan and his son Ezra and they looked in no pleasant mood. 'Morning, gentlemen,' said Bates, 'how can I be helping you all?'

'Cut the small talk, Bates,' said the elder Mr Doolan roughly, 'I ain't in the right frame of mind to appreciate it.'

'Well then, what can I do for you?'

'You can issue a warrant for the Armstrongs on a charge of murder and conspiracy to murder,' was the surprising reply. Sheriff Bates knew then that his life had just got a whole lot more complicated and that having the cavalry riding through town was likely to be among the least of his troubles.

5

While Sheriff Brewster was trying to calm down what promised to turn into the most awkward fix he had ever been in since he was appointed sheriff of Parson's End, the four Armstrong brothers were talking over the best way they knew to protect their parents from further harm. Seth Armstrong's wound looked, at least to Anthony's eyes, to be healing up nicely, but their father was in no fit state to be moved. Since their mother wouldn't dream of being separated from her husband, this meant that their plans revolved around defending the house from possible attack.

Soon after Jack had come in from the barn that morning, Anthony had contrived to speak to him privately, without Tom and Andrew hearing. He said, 'Jack, it might be life or death for us, you have to level with me. Do you think you killed anybody for sure last night?'

His brother nodded reluctantly and then shook his head in despair. Anthony said, 'You certain sure about it?'

'I shot Mrs Doolan in the face. I saw the ball strike her full in the face; she's dead all right.'

Anthony shook his head. He was genuinely grieved to hear of the woman's death; after all, he had been speaking to her in such a friendly fashion not twenty-four hours earlier. Still, that was nothing to the purpose. The only thing now was to make sure that they came out on top if there was to be any sort of a rough-house. So woebegone did his brother look that Anthony reached over and squeezed Jack's shoulder reassuringly, saying, 'Hey, it'll be fine. You'll see.'

This little kindness was ill-received by his brother, who jerked away irritably and said, 'You ain't my pa! The hell gives you the right to put on airs so? You ain't been home above five minutes and you're throwing your weight round.'

This was not at all how Anthony

thought he had been behaving, but he had the grace to mutter an apology. It was plain to him that Jack nursed some kind of grudge, about what, though, he knew nothing.

It was agreed that they should all four of them go armed at all times and that other business should be suspended for the time being. Anthony suggested that a good plan might be for one of them to remain in the house and a second to be concealed in the barn, so as to be able, as he put it, 'to provide flanking fire'. His brother Tom shot him a quizzical look when his baby brother lapsed into military jargon in this way. Nevertheless, he agreed in principle with what his brother had proposed. All four thought it best if two of them rode patrol around their land so that they would see anybody approaching long before they reached the house.

It was two years since he had so much as touched a firearm, but there wasn't a great deal of purpose in going on the scout without one. When he had returned from the war, Anthony had wrapped up the pistol he had carried for two years and stuck in back of the old closet in the room he had shared with Andrew as a child. His rifle he had already disposed of by the simple expedient of abandoning it on the train as he headed home.

The pistol was still where he had left it, wrapped in an old duster at the bottom of a tin box, in which as a boy he used to hide his treasures. It was a Metropolitan Arms copy of the 1861 Colt Navy and it had cost him a small fortune in 1863. When once he'd signed up, he had figured that it would be wise to buy the best sidearm he could afford and it had taken a good chunk of the money that he had been carrying to see him through the Michaelmas term at Harvard. It had been a good investment, though; there were those who said that the Metropolitan's version of the Navy Colt was a better weapon than the original.

Having collected his gun, Anthony

went down to the kitchen to join the others, who were fiddling around with ramrods, cleaning brushes and little cans of oil, making sure that their weapons were in tip-top condition in case their lives depended upon them. Indeed, a misfire during a gun battle could easily make the difference between life and death. Tom shifted to one side, making room for Anthony. The other three watched him curiously as he tapped out the wedge which held the barrel in place and began cleaning and oiling the weapon.

'I reckon that's a thing you don't get up to much out East,' observed Tom.

'Cleaning and loading a pistol?' replied Anthony, 'no, you have a point there. Still, needs must when the Devil drives. You know where Ma keeps the bacon fat?'

'In that jar over yonder,' said Andrew, 'the little blue one.'

Anthony got up and went over to the shelf. He took the jar and then scooped out a small amount of the congealed, white fat on the tip of his finger. When he was seated again, he smeared this around the front of the chambers. Seeing his brothers' inquiring looks, he said, 'Little trick I learned. Smear of grease like this catches any sparks when you fire. Stops having one shot setting off another in the neighbouring chamber.'

'Lordy,' said Andrew, 'it is a pure pleasure to hear the way you talk these days. You sounded a cut above us after them lessons with the minister, but it's nothing to how you are since you been at college.'

'I'm the same person I ever was,' said Anthony, a little stiffly.

Before riding out with Tom, Anthony went in quietly to speak to his mother and father. His father was sitting up in the bed and looking as though he was going to pull through with no difficulty. Martha sat at her husband's side, holding his hand. This was such an unusual display of affection that the young man could not help but stare at the sight. This prompted his mother to observe tartly, 'What are you lookin' at, hey? Think there's something unnatural 'bout a wife touching her husband so?'

'No, not a bit of it, Ma,' he replied. 'It's not common to see you and my pa so, that's all.'

His mother sniffed, saying, 'Well if you and those rascally brothers of yours hadn't been out raising Cain, we wouldn't be in this fix and there'd be no occasion for me to be fooling around in this way. I'd be in the kitchen cooking or out in God's open air tending my garden. Anyways, what's the news?'

Before her son could reply, Seth said sharply, 'You're sportin' iron. That ain't what I'd o' hoped to see, not by a long chalk. What are you about?'

Anthony outlined the arrangements that he and his brothers had made before turning to his father and asking, 'That sound good to you, sir?'

His father smiled and replied, 'It's a good long spell since I was in the army, boy. Happen you're the best one to figure things of that kind. It sorrows me, though, to see you drawn into this nonsense.'

'Are you feeling any better today?'

'I ain't as young as once I was. When I was your age, Anthony, I took a ball in my shoulder and didn't even lay up the next day. Just carried on fighting. Now? Just a little nick like this is enough to lay me low. Don't grow old, boy, it ain't a heap o' fun, I'll tell you that for nothing.'

'Maybe it's better than the alternative,' said Anthony soberly. His father thought this over for a moment before bursting into laughter; a deep, rich belly laugh which caused his wife to say anxiously,

'Lord, Seth, hush up, you old fool. You're going to bust those stitches loose directly!'

'Better than the alternative,' said Seth Armstrong. 'Yes, I like that. You got that right, boy.'

'Get along out of here now, son,' said Martha, 'I want this man to rest and you're purely creating a disturbance.'

In the kitchen, the other three brothers heard the old man laughing and exchanged meaningful looks. Their father never roared with laughter in that way at anything that they ever said or did.

★ ★ ★

Two things were as plain as pikestaffs to Brewster Bates. The first was that any dream he had entertained of coasting along in this job until he was able to retire in a few years, respected and wealthy, were fast vanishing over the horizon. The second was that there was going to be bloodshed before very long. The sheriff had tried to prevaricate and fob the Doolans off with soft words and then figure out later what to do about the situation, but they were having none of it.

'My wife's lying dead back at my house, Bates,' said Doolan in a soft, but deadly, voice. 'You taken my money over the years, well now I want the value of it.'

'I don't rightly know what you'd have me do,' said Sheriff Bates hopelessly. 'It's not what I would call a clearcut case.'

'Not clearcut?' interrupted Ezra. 'What the hell are you talkin' about, you fat bastard?'

Michael Doolan held up his hand to calm down his son. When the young man had stumbled to a halt, Doolan looked Brewster Bates straight in the eye and said, 'You listen to what I say now and listen good. I know fine well it was one of the Armstrongs who killed my Susan and so do you. I don't know which o' them it was, but they's all in it up to their necks. You don't ride out there this day and find the men who came by my house last night, then I'll deal with this my way. But I tell you, Bates, that happen and you'll wish you was never born.' Without waiting for any reply, Michael Doolan signalled to his son and the two men walked out of the sheriff's office without uttering another word.

After the Doolans had left, Bates found that he was running with sweat. It was trickling down his chest and coated his forehead in an uncomfortable slick. He had sensed that it would not have taken much for the two men to explode in violence and he was glad that that at least had been averted. That Mrs Doolan was dead seemed certain. The idea that one of the Armstrongs had shot her, though, didn't ring at all true to Brewster Bates. The devil of it was of course that he was also beholden to the Armstrongs, whose cash he had been taking for years in just the way that he had been paid by the Doolans. With a heavy heart, Sheriff Bates stood up and left his office, locking the door behind him. At the very least, he supposed that he would have to ride over to the Armstrongs' and see what they had to say about this. It was not an interview to which he was looking forward.

Tom and Anthony saw the lone rider approaching from the direction of town and at once changed tack to intercept the man. When they saw that it was Sheriff Bates, they relaxed a little, knowing that he was practically on the payroll of their family. 'Hey, Brewster,' called Tom, 'how's it going, man?'

'Not so good, not so good at all, Tom, I had Mr Doolan and his boy Ezra come to see me this morning. You know his wife's dead?'

'Susan Doolan dead?' exclaimed Tom in amazement, 'Lord, no. What happened?'

'She was shot.'

'How's that?' asked Anthony, playing his own part in the game. 'An accident or what?'

'It was no accident,' said Bates, eyeing both men closely for signs that they were dissembling with him. 'Three men rode up to his place last night and murdered her.'

'Murder?' said Anthony. 'You see the body yet, Sheriff?'

'Not yet. Why d'you ask?'

Anthony shrugged in an embarrassed way, as though diffident at putting forward his view. 'Most killings are done by family members. Husbands, sons and suchlike. I just would have thought that you'd look into the circumstances before taking a man's word about such a thing.'

Now it has to be said that Sheriff Brewster Bates was not the smartest man in the Arizona Territory; even his best friend would not have described him as being sharp as a lancet. He was, however, shrewd, with an animal cunning, and looking now at the two young men sitting there watching him carefully, Bates suddenly knew without the shadow of a doubt that they were stringing him along and knew somewhat more about this business than they were letting on.

At the moment that Bates realized that he was being lied to, he happened to look into Tom Armstrong's face and knew that Armstrong was aware that he didn't believe a word of what he was saying. It was an awkward moment for all parties concerned, but Bates knew that there might yet be something worse than awkwardness. Both Tom and Anthony were wearing pistols and in addition, Tom had a sawn-off scattergun slung over his shoulder. There was a hard look about both of them, which gave Bates to suppose that if pushed, they would not hesitate to use violence. He said casually, 'Well, maybe you're right at that. Happen I ought to look in at the Doolan place and see what I can find out there.'

Anthony said quietly, 'I think that would be the smart dodge, Sheriff.'

'Well, I'll be by later to talk some more to you boys, if that's agreeable?'

'Sure thing, Sheriff,' said Tom, all amiability. 'You come by for a coffee or something. I know my pa'd be right glad to see you.'

After Bates had ridden off, Anthony said to his brother, 'He knows we're lying, I suppose you know that?'

Tom laughed. 'Sure he knows. He's a bag of wind and piss. He ain't a-goin' to do aught about it.'

'Maybe not, but if he won't, then Mr Doolan will. Whether the man who shot his wife is hanged or whether he's shot down, Doolan will want his blood. One way or another, there's a fight coming on us.'

'You ain't 'fraid of a fight, are you, baby brother?'

Anthony looked coldly at his brother and said, 'I'm not afeared of anything. I'm just telling you how it will be.'

* * *

As they rode home from town, Mick Doolan said nothing and his son didn't like to interrupt whatever chain of thought his pa was following. At length, Ezra asked, 'You think Bates is going to go out and arrest the Armstrongs, Pa?'

'Wouldn't o' thought so at all,' came the answer.

'So why'd we go to him then?'

'So's I can tell anybody later that we tried the lawful route first, before going down the other road.'

'You got plans then, Pa?'

'You might say so. I want whoever shot your ma strung up. An' hanging alongside him, I want anybody as aided and abetted him, or knew what he was planning or helped him or covered up for him. I want every man who was in anywise mixed up in that killing to pay for it. If it means spillin' every drop of my own blood, I'll be avenged for this.'

Ezra said nothing, wondering how this would all pan out. Then his father asked, 'How many o' them fellows as works with us could we rely on, if the knife meets the bone?'

'You mean the hired hands or the men living nigh to us?'

'Both.'

'That Hogan's as hard as they come. Always providin' we pay him enough, I reckon he'll stick at naught. Then there's the Carters. Him and his boys's mighty handy. We can rely on them.

And Bill Travers, I should say we can count him in.'

'I come up with the same names myself. Add us and that gives us eight to take care of this. Might not be enough, not if them Armstrongs can rustle up help. This needs thinking on.'

Ezra Doolan, who was not precisely soft himself, was struck by his father's iron determination and complete lack of outward show of grief. He himself had shed a few tears in the privacy of his room, but apart from that brief display of feeling immediately after his wife was shot, his father gave the impression simply of a man with a little job of work to accomplish. God help the Armstrongs, thought Ezra, they surely don't know what's about to hit them.

Tim Hogan was a very worried man. In a straight fight he was not scared of anything or anyone. He had only been beaten once or twice in fistfights and never at all when guns had been involved. But he was feeling distinctly uneasy on this early afternoon. The cause of his anxiety was simple. Mick Doolan was on the vengeance trail and swearing to kill with his own two hands any man who had any part, no matter how trifling, in the death of his beloved wife. No excuses would serve; there would be no reasoning with him. Once before, Hogan had seen a man in this state of lust for revenge and on that occasion it had ended in the deaths of a dozen people. The man concerned, though, had taken his vengeance, even though it ultimately cost him his own life. In his waters, Hogan felt that this was a similar case and he was thinking hard of a way to extricate himself from the trap into which he had fallen.

He had nobody but his own self to thank for the predicament in which he currently found himself. There'd been no need at all to start shooting at the Armstrong boy. After all, what had it been about? A punch on the jaw and a little joshing from his fellow workers. It was nothing; less than nothing. But it had been enough to set in motion the chain of events which had ended in Susan Doolan's killing and if old man Doolan found out, then he was as good as dead.

The obvious thing to do was what Tim Hogan had always done when things became a little tricky: dig up and run. That wouldn't answer in the present case, because at the first sign of anything that looked like guilt, which is what flight would inevitably suggest to Mick Doolan in his present state, the Doolans and their associates would be putting together a posse and hunting him down. No, he'd do better to stay and bluff it out. But one question was nagging away at his mind. Had either old Seth Armstrong or that damned son of his actually caught sight of Hogan? If they had, then the fact was sure to come out at some point and his role in precipitating the violence would be out of the bag.

It was a regular conundrum and Hogan decided in the end to solve it in the way that he invariably solved such puzzles: by the use of bloody violence. In short, he took it into his head to kill the Armstrongs, father and son, thus covering his tracks once for all.

* * *

After turning tail from Tom and Anthony Armstrong, Sheriff Bates thought that he might as well go on to Doolan's place, although the good Lord knew that this was anything but an attractive prospect. He didn't see, though, that he had any other choice; if he didn't report what had happened, then Mr Doolan would be coming after him and the way that gentleman had been when last they met, Bates didn't especially relish the idea of Mick Doolan being ticked off with him. He was received contemptuously by the Doolans.

'They run you off their land, is that the strength of it?' asked Ezra, when the sheriff had given a halting and shame-faced account of his visit to the

Armstrongs. 'You just turned tail and ran.'

'No, I wouldn't o' — ' began the wretched man, when Michael Doolan interrupted him, saying,

'You ain't up to the job. Well then, I am. You just take care to stand aside and make sure you don't interfere. You got that straight?'

'I guess . . . ' said Brewster Bates miserably. 'You got to see how I'm placed.'

'Get out of my sight, you son of a bitch!' said Mick Doolan suddenly, tiring of the fellow. 'Just recollect what you been told. Stand aside and don't concern yourself with anything.'

6

That night, the second after Anthony Armstrong returned from Massachusetts, three men died near Parson's End. This is what happened.

Just after dark, Mick Doolan sat down with his two sons, Joe having by that time returned, and between them they laid their plans. Since they were only likely to muster eight men in total and the Armstrongs might be in a position to get together at least as many, the elder Mr Doolan decided to tilt the odds in his favour a little by scaring off one or two potential supporters of the men with whom he aimed to have a reckoning. After talking the matter over with his sons, it was agreed that Jed Stone and his friend Albert were weak types who would most likely be amenable to a little pressure. They weren't hard men, making their living chiefly by the production and sale of intoxicating liquor. Michael Doolan thought that if a half dozen men paid them a friendly visit and gave them a warning, they would go to ground for a while and reduce the numbers on the Armstrongs' side.

Jed Stone had his brewing apparatus and still set up in an outbuilding, which had started life as a stone-built pig pen. He had built up the walls a little and fashioned a new roof out of brushwood and the little hut, not much bigger than a privy, functioned perfectly well as his brew house. He was fooling around in there a couple of hours after sunset when he heard the thunder of hoofs. Unless he missed his guess, there must have been at least six or seven riders coming in his direction. Stone picked up the storm lantern, by whose light he had been working, and went out to see who it was.

The horrible events of the previous night had not troubled either Jed or

Albert too badly. They were phlegmatic and unimaginative types, who had seen people killed before that night. Anyway, it hadn't been them who had pulled the trigger and, at a pinch, they had agreed with each other they could always turn State's evidence and give away Jack Armstrong. Not that they really thought there would be any sort of consequence from what had been done. Like most other folk thereabouts, they viewed Sheriff Bates with good-natured contempt, thinking it exceedingly unlikely that he would be able to bring home the crime to them.

The six men who rode up were obviously not part of a law posse, which was the only thing that Stone really feared. He recognized Mick Doolan and his two sons, but Brewster Bates was nowhere in evidence. It stood to reason that Doolan was likely to be aggrieved about the loss of his wife, but even so, Jed Stone failed to realize fully his peril. He said brightly, 'Good evenin', Mr Doolan. What brings you out here? You lost your way?' Had he but known it, nothing was more calculated to rile the recently widowed man than this perky and light-hearted air.

'I'm here to speak to you, Stone,' said Doolan, 'And you best listen good to what I say.'

Now at this point, of course, all that Doolan was aiming for was to discourage Albert and Jed from riding against them on behalf of the Armstrongs. It was Albert who made the mortal mistake of coming out of the house and misreading the situation. He took the band of riders for a lynch mob, ready to exact vengeance for the killing of the woman the night before. He shouted in a panic-stricken voice, anxious to save his own neck, 'Hell it weren't us as opened fire. Tell him, Jed. It was that damned fool, young Armstrong.'

'Shut your mouth, for Christ's sake,' Stone yelled back at him, appalled by his partner's words. 'They ain't inquiring 'bout nothing.'

Doolan's eyes narrowed, but of course nobody saw that in the gloom. He said, 'Who said aught about opening fire, hey? What d'you boys have to tell me?'

'Don't you set any store by what Albert here says,' said Stone, trying desperately to keep his voice level and relaxed. 'He's been at our latest batch of poteen. It's powerful strong and he don't know what he's saying after a glass or two. You want that I should draw you some to try? All you men are welcome, of course.' He smiled in a ghastly attempt to appear relaxed and sociable and not give the impression of a man in fear of his very life.

Doolan said to his sons, 'Cover those bastards and shoot them if they offer any resistance. Don't kill 'em, though. Just put a ball in their belly or something. I want to hear the tale they got to tell.'

'It's not what you think,' Albert said, as Ezra and Joe Doolan dismounted and advanced upon him and Jed. 'We

110

was there, but we didn't do nothing. It was that Jack as did it.'

'Did what?' asked Doolan in a pleasant and friendly voice. 'Tell me what Jack Armstrong did.'

Realizing that the game was up, and inwardly cursing his friend for every sort of fool, Jed Stone spoke up, saying, 'Here's the way of it, Mr Doolan. Jack came by here last night and asked us to come out to your place. He swore he meant you no harm and we was just goin' to put a fright in you. That's right, ain't it, Bert?'

'Yeah, God's honest truth, sir. We asked him, we said, 'There ain't a goin' to be no shooting?' and he says to us, 'Not a bit of it, boys. Just scaring 'em.''

'So you just went with him and it was he as fired the shot, that's the long and the short of it, hey?' asked Doolan in a voice which was friendly and encouraging.

'That's it, yeah. That's all,' said Stone. 'We never would o' come if we'd o' suspicioned that he meant mischief, would we, Albert?'

'Hell no. We ain't that type at all, you know that, Mr Doolan.'

'Sure,' said Doolan softly, 'I know that.' He turned to the men at his side and said, 'Hang them. They was part of it.'

'But you can't,' cried Albert in terror, 'you can't hang us for just being there. It ain't . . . it ain't just!'

'Hang them!' repeated Doolan.

Both men died hard, kicking out their lives at the end of the ropes, which Doolan and his men had thoughtfully made sure to bring with them, just on the off-chance that they would be needed. When Stone and his friend were dead, Doolan directed his men to torch the cabin and smash up the still, spilling all the moonshine on the ground. It seemed like a wicked waste to the other men, but it was clear that this was neither the time nor the place to get crosswise to the old man.

Tim Hogan, one of the party which hanged the two moonshiners, exulted as they were strung up from the tree which grew by their cabin. Perhaps these deaths would go some way to assuaging his employer's wrath. Even so, he thought that it would still be a smart move to silence Seth Armstrong and the fellow he now knew was his youngest son. The mood that Doolan was in and the ruthless way that he had disposed of the two men hanged that night were confirmation that running off would be the worst possible move for Hogan to make. No, he'd best try to kill those Armstrongs without telling anybody and then be sure to stay alongside that mad bastard Doolan as he wrought whatever other vengeance he had in mind.

As far as Michael Doolan was concerned, they had done a good night's work. He dismissed the men who had ridden with him and helped to hang Jed and Albert. 'It won't be forgot,' he told these men before they left to go to their homes. 'I owe you boys a big debt and I'm a man who believes in paying his obligations. I'll recollect what you done for me this day, never fear.'

As he rode home with his sons, Doolan asked them, 'Well, how d'you read it? You think Jack Armstrong acted on his own?'

'Without his pa knowing of it?' asked Ezra, 'I wouldn't o' said so. What d'you think, Joe?'

'No, not in a thousand years. Mark what I say, this was Seth Armstrong and his boys together. Jack was sent.'

'That's pretty much the way I figure it too,' said their father. 'That Jack, he's not the one to take on a job like that, not 'less he was instructed in it.'

The three of them rode on for a while in silence, before Joe Doolan said, 'So what's next, Pa? We take Jack Armstrong by his self? Or you want that we take out the whole nest of 'em and burn down their house?'

'I'm goin' to think on it, son. But we ain't doing anything more 'til your ma, God rest her, is decently buried. Then we'll have us a reckoning.'

After Tim Hogan and the other men separated from the Doolans, he waited a decent interval before announcing his intention to go to town, claiming that he had an assignation with some girl. The killing of Jed Stone and Albert had sobered all those who had had a hand in the affair and Hogan's news was not greeted with the usual ribaldry that any mention of a young woman might have been expected to produce. Instead, the others just grunted and carried on their way when Hogan split off and headed across country in the general direction of Parson's End.

There wasn't what you might call a definite plan in Hogan's head; several possibilities had presented themselves to him. One of these was that the family would still be up and about, but indoors, moving about in a relaxed fashion. If that was the case, then he might be able to creep up to the house, smash a window and start shooting in at the men he hoped to kill. If that was to be how things went, then he could jump on his horse afterwards and then gallop off before anybody had a chance even to get their horses saddled up. Another, but less attractive idea entailed scouting round and then coming back the following night and hiding near the house. Then, when the men he was seeking came out early in the morning, he could gun them down unawares. His trip to the Armstrong house was really a probing exercise, to see what the best way of accomplishing his end might be.

As it happened, Tim Hogan didn't have the opportunity to put into execution either of the tentative schemes he was hatching. As he rode across the fields which surrounded the Armstrongs' house, he had no idea that he was already under observation. Andrew Armstrong was patrolling the hayloft of the barn which stood near the house, constantly scanning in all directions to make sure that nobody would take them by surprise. It had been agreed with his brothers that a rifle shot would be the signal that a number of men were coming down on the house. If it was just one man, though, he had said that he'd play it by ear.

Cradled in his arms, Andrew had a Sharp's 0.52 carbine, which he had picked up after the war from a discharged soldier. He was a rare shot with this weapon, using it principally for hunting game for the pot. The barn was becoming more than a little dilapidated and there were planks missing or rotted in half on all points of the compass. This meant that Andrew could stroll from side to side, peering out into the night. His ears were keen and he knew that he'd be able to pick up the sound of horses long before he saw them. It was while he was looking north that he heard the sound of a horse cantering through the darkness. It was, as far as Andrew could gauge, a mile from him.

This was the second curious incident of Andrew's lonely watch. Maybe a half hour earlier, he had become aware of a ruddy glow above the hills to the east. If he was any judge of such matters, then he would say that there was a pretty large fire raging over in that direction and since there were no forests out that way, this probably meant that some poor devil's house was burning. It was hard to be sure, but at a guess, Andrew would say that the blaze was right where he'd place Jed Stone's cabin. He had a terrible foreboding that the fighting had already begun while he was walking about up here in the hay loft. He only hoped that neither Tom nor Anthony was caught up in it. But then if that had been the case, surely he would have heard the sound of shooting?

The sound of the thudding hoofs in the distance stopped abruptly and Andrew strained to see if he could catch any sound from that direction. Then he caught the plodding rhythm of a horse walking, but still coming towards him. This was exceedingly suspicious and he tried to reason out the case to himself. It surely wasn't Anthony and

Tom, because they were staying together. If some emergency had arisen and one or the other of the pair were returning to the house alone, then they would have no reason to suddenly slow down like that. It suggested, to Andrew's alert mind, subterfuge and cunning. He pulled back the hammer of the Sharp's and pointed it into the darkness.

According to Hogan's reckoning, the Armstrong house should be just over the next rise of ground. It was a pity that there was only a crescent moon; it made it difficult to pick out detail. But there, the house was a half mile ahead of him. His sense of direction hadn't played him false. There were lamps lit in two of the windows, which gave him to hope that his idea of shooting folk through the window might just come off. He certainly hoped so, because the sooner he managed to kill Seth Armstrong and his youngest son, the sooner he would sleep easy in his own bed.

Uncertain though the light was, Andrew saw the shadowy silhouette of a rider coming over the crest. There was only one man, which to his mind ruled out its being one of his brothers. As he watched, the man dismounted and began to walk his horse straight towards the barn. Resting his rifle on the plank which delineated the bottom of one of the holes in the wall of the barn, Andrew Armstrong squinted down the barrel. It was hopeless; he could barely see anything in this light. He would just have to hope and pray that whoever was walking slowly in the direction of the house stopped for a spell, so that he could get a proper bead on him.

It wasn't until he was nearly at the barn, which loomed up ahead of him, that Hogan knew for sure what he had it in mind to do. He wondered why he hadn't thought of it before. He would set a fire at the side of the Armstrong house, wait 'til the occupants came running out to deal with it and then shoot them down. He smiled in the darkness at the idea. Well, it would do no harm at all to pause for a minute to have a smoke before putting the scheme into execution. Luckily, he had the makings about him. Hogan took out his tobacco pouch and fumbled around for papers. When he'd rolled the cigarette, he fished around for a lucifer and then lit it with his thumbnail. Just as the flaring, sulphurous blue flame illuminated his face, destroying his night vision, a voice came from right overhead. 'Throw down your weapons if you want to live!'

Much as Tim Hogan wished to live, he trusted no living man to keep his word and so, rather than putting up his hands or anything of that kind, he made to pull his rifle from where it reposed in the buckskin scabbard at the front of the saddle. His hand never even touched the weapon before there was a sharp crack overhead and a ball passed down through his chest, shattering the collarbone on the way, before rupturing his heart. He was, to all intents and purposes, dead by the time he hit the ground.

Two miles away, Anthony and Tom Armstrong heard the shot and reined in, hoping that their ears had deceived them and they were neither of them right in supposing that the shot had come from the direction of their home. It was already plain to the pair of them that there was mischief afoot that night. Like Andrew, they had seen the flickering light over towards Jed Stone's place. They had been making their way cautiously in that direction when they heard the shot.

'What d'you say?' asked Tom. 'Think that came from the house?'

'I'd say so,' replied his brother. 'We best get back.'

'I'm mighty glad that Andrew and Jack are there, keeping an eye on Ma and Pa.'

They turned and began trotting their horses homewards. There was no percentage in cantering, let alone galloping through the pitch darkness that enveloped them. The fact that there had been no more shooting encouraged them to think that Andrew had simply signalled them, as agreed, by firing into the air. With luck, they would be there in time to lend a hand with whatever it was that had alarmed their brother.

Jack came haring out of the house, holding a pistol in one hand and a storm lantern in the other. Andrew called down, 'Mind what you're about. Don't you go shooting me when I come down.'

'What's to do? Somebody coming?'

'Not any more,' replied his brother dryly. 'Come, shed a little light round the other side o' the barn.'

They found Tim Hogan lying dead. His mare had at first been spooked by the gunfire, but had now returned and was nudging at the corpse with her head. 'You recognize him?' asked Andrew.

'Yeah, that's Hogan. He's the one that Anthony said he had a run-in with,

123

day he stepped off the stage. He's Doolan's man.'

Andrew, who was a little near-sighted, bent down and peered harder at the corpse. 'So it is! Well, that's no great loss.'

The two of them were dragging Hogan's body into the barn when Anthony and Tom rode up. Having apprised them of the situation, Anthony said, 'Either of you two see flames over yonder? Nigh to Jed Stone's cabin?'

'I saw 'em,' said Andrew. 'Figured it was Stone's place as well. You think Mick Doolan might o' paid him a visit?'

'I'd call it a racing certainty,' said Anthony soberly.

By now, Martha Armstrong had come out to see what all the fuss was about. Anthony noted with amusement that his mother had a little muff pistol clutched in her hand. She said, 'Well, you boys kill somebody or what?'

'It's not a pretty sight, Ma,' said Anthony gently, 'you best let us handle it.'

'Pretty sight, nothing,' she said irritably. 'Who is it? One of the Doolan boys?'

'No, it's one of their hands.'

Their mother walked a little way into the barn and stared dispassionately at the corpse lying there on the dusty floor. 'Well, I hope you ain't aimin' for to leave it there for good,' she remarked. 'Last I heard killing folk is still against the law. You don't want to leave evidence all over the place.'

'We'll deal with it tomorrow,' said Tom admiringly. Like his brothers, he never ceased to be amazed at his mother and the reserves of common sense and courage she brought forth whenever necessary. 'How's Pa?'

'On the mend. He wants to go by Michael Doolan's house to make the peace.'

'God almighty,' exclaimed Anthony in horror. 'It's not to be thought of. I hope you told him so?'

'Never mind taking the Lord's name in vain,' said his mother, 'of course I told him. I ain't sure he completely knows what's happened.' She turned and went back into the house.

Tom said, 'We're goin' to have to fix this up, 'fore Pa's up and about. One way or another, we got to put a stop to this business.'

'I thought I'd ride over to Jed tomorrow,' said Anthony, 'see if we're right about that fire. Then I guess I'd better go into town and speak to that famous sheriff of ours.'

'Brewster? What the hell d'you think that useless article can do to help?' asked Andrew.

'I don't know. Nothing, most likely. But I'm worried that if things go on down this road, then there's no telling what the result will be.'

7

The next morning, Anthony and Tom rode over to Jed Stone's place to see if they had been right about the source of the previous night's fire. Although they were quite prepared to find his cabin a smouldering ruin, they were both taken aback to find the two bodies swaying gently in the morning breeze.

'Jeez,' said Tom, 'that's the hell of a thing. I never expected they'd go that far.'

Anthony shrugged and then dismounted. He said, 'What would you have? Mr Doolan was dead set on finding out who killed his wife. Can't say as I blame him. She was a wonderful, sweet woman.'

Tom Armstrong stared at his brother for a few seconds without saying anything. Then he ventured, 'You ain't backing out on us, are you? I mean you're still with us on this?'

'I'm with you and the others to the death. But that doesn't mean I'm not sorry about what befell Susan Doolan. Tell me, what dealings did you have with these boys?'

'They took care of horses for us. Why?'

'You know where they kept them?'

Tom looked puzzled. 'Yeah, little gully away up there.'

Anthony rubbed his chin thoughtfully and said, 'I'm going to take these bodies into town and set them down outside Brewster Bates' office. I want to show people where things are heading and make sure that they know it's not all our doing, the killing and so on, I mean.'

'Don't see the good o' that.'

'Bates might be a useless fool, but he's still the law. If folk see that he's not up to dealing with this sort of thing, then they might not take it so ill when we take our own action. After all, you fellows got to go on living here even after I've gone back to law school.'

Tom thought this over and then said, 'Meaning you think we're going to end up in a shooting match with the Doolans?'

'What else? You think a man's going to see his wife shot through the face and die in front of him and then not seek to kill all those who were mixed up in it? Listen, he hanged these two; you got to know that he's got Jack's name. You want we should hand over our brother to Mr Doolan?'

'Hell no!'

'Well then, we have to be ready to defend him. You asked if I was backing out, I might say the same to you. This isn't going to end with both us and the Doolans still standing.'

Hearing the setup laid out so plain sent an involuntary shiver through Tom Armstrong's frame. He was no sort of coward, but nor did he relish getting into a fight to the death with a bunch of determined men like this. He said to his brother, 'You got the lion's share of the brains in this here family. Can't you see any way out of this?'

'Not when it's got this far, I can't.'

Andrew and Jack were surprised and not a little disconcerted when their two brothers fetched up back at the house with two ponies in tow, on each of which was roped a dead body. Because they were both hanging face down, the identities of the corpses were not immediately apparent. Andrew said, 'Where'd you pick them up? It ain't any of the Doolans, I suppose?'

Jack went up and took a closer look at the bodies, lifting each head up by the hair and peering into their faces. He turned to Andrew and said, 'It's not Doolans. This here's Jed Stone and his partner.'

'What's the game?' asked Andrew. When Anthony had outlined his thinking, Andrew nodded slowly, saying, 'There's sense in the scheme, I'll allow. Else Mick Doolan'll be putting it all around town that we're a bunch o' man-killers and he's pure as the driven snow. It's a smart idea.'

Turning to Jack, Anthony said, 'You can bet what you will that these two told Doolan before they died who fired the shot that killed his wife. I don't think you'd better show your face in town until we've dealt with this, once and for all.'

Jack looked disposed to argue the point, taking it ill that his younger brother should attempt to set a limit upon his movement in this way, but both Tom and Andrew chipped in and told him that he shouldn't stir far from the house.

Before he set off for town, Anthony said, 'We'll be wanting to get shot of that body in the barn. I was thinking of that old sinkhole, away over towards the river. The one we used to say was bottomless.'

'Yes,' said Tom, 'that's the very thing. We'll see to it while you're away. You sure you want to go alone? Wouldn't rather make it a family trip?'

'I can handle myself. I don't need help.' The quiet and confident way that this was said might have sounded like boasting or bravado coming from another man. His brothers, though, knew that Anthony was stating no more than the simple and unadorned truth. He very likely *could* handle anything by his own self.

★   ★   ★

Michael Doolan rode into Parson's End early that morning with his son Ezra, leaving Joe to take charge of matters at the house. He knew that it was time to make arrangements for his wife's funeral.

There were only two churches in Parson's End; the Presbytarian and the Catholic. The Doolans were, in name at least, Catholic and it was accordingly to Father Docherty's house alongside the church that they directed their steps when they reached town. The rumour was already circulating about Susan

Doolan's untimely death and so Father Docherty was not all that surprised to see the Doolans, father and son, walking up his path. His housekeeper opened the door and showed the visitors into the parlour.

Michael Doolan was not a man to waste words in pointless parley. He said to the priest, 'You know why we're here?'

'I can guess. It'll be about your poor dear wife.'

'Yes, she was a regular worshipper at your church, Father. I'm hoping that you can give her a fine send-off.'

The elderly priest made a clicking noise with his tongue, suggestive of irritation. 'I wouldn't know what you mean by a fine send-off, Mr Doolan. I'll certainly be glad to give a good, Catholic mother and wife a Christian burial, if that's what you're asking.'

'It is.'

'Well then, will tomorrow suit or would you be wanting time to invite relatives from further afield?'

'Tomorrow will be grand.'

Neither Michael Doolan nor his son had shown any inclination to sit. Nor did they display any desire to stay longer, now that the business had been taken care of. Father Docherty, though, had a few words that he wished to say and he did so without more ado. He said, 'I'm hearing a story that you might be seeking vengeance for your wife's death. I'm hopeful that there's not a word of truth in such a tale?'

Neither of the men standing before him replied. Father Docherty continued, 'You'll be recollecting what the Good Book teaches us about private vengeance? It never tends to the good. Your wife was a God-fearing woman and I'll be honoured to conduct the rites for to inter her. But I can tell the both of you now that if you go straight from the mass for your wife's repose with murder in your hearts, then you'll be in a state of mortal sin. Do you hear what I say?'

'What time can you carry out the

funeral tomorrow?' asked Michael Doolan, his face impassive.

'Would one o'clock be agreeable? Will you see that your wife's remains are conveyed here early in the morning?'

When the two Doolans had left the house, Father Docherty stood by the window, watching them walk down the path and towards Main Street. If ever there was a man determined upon bloody revenge, he thought to himself, then that man is Michael Doolan, God rest his soul.

The arrival in town of Anthony Armstrong, accompanied by two corpses, caused something of a stir in Parson's End. So far, the only thing that was known in the town was that Susan Doolan had been killed, allegedly by the Armstrongs, or somebody acting on their behalf. This at least was the story that had been doing the rounds among drinkers at the Lucky Lady. Brewster Bates had intimated as much to one or two associates and they had spread the news far and wide. Mrs Doolan had been a popular figure in town, always about some charitable work or other and news of her murder had created a certain amount of indignation. All else apart, the killing of any woman was regarded with loathing and detestation. Now, it appeared that there might be another side to the matter.

Anthony Armstrong had always been seen as the most respectable of the Armstrong boys and seeing him walking his horse down Main Street with two ponies following him, each laden with a dead body, was no common sight. People called each other out of stores to come and see the strange spectacle. When he reached the sheriff's office, Anthony reined in his horse and dismounted. Then, in a leisurely and unhurried manner, he pulled a knife from his saddle-bag and cut the ropes securing the bodies onto the back of the ponies. Having done this, he picked up first one corpse and then another, setting them down neatly on the sidewalk, right outside Brewster Bates' office.

Anybody hoping to walk along the boardwalk past the sheriff's office would now be obliged either to step over two corpses or make a detour into the road.

A small crowd gathered to watch this singular event; they stood there in the road as though this was some sort of entertainment, like a circus act. The corpses of Jed Stone and Albert Donague presented a ghastly aspect; their faces were blackened and engorged with blood. It was plain that they had died hard. When he was sure that nobody walking down Main Street would be likely to pass by without becoming aware of the late lamented moonshiners, Anthony addressed the group of spectators.

'You folk might have been hearing a lot of lies about my family. Well, here's the truth of it. Those two men, neighbours of ours and good friends, were lynched last night. My own father is lying in bed this minute, his life in the balance, because some cowardly assassin shot him down while he was tending to his own business on his own land. Me and my family aren't the villains here. We just want to get on with our lives, but we won't let anybody push us around either. I'm telling you all that we want peace, but if we're pushed, we'll fight back.'

This speech had a great effect on those who heard it. Nobody had ever heard any bad of young Anthony Armstrong and if what he said was true, then perhaps they had been a little hasty to take at face value what the Doolans were putting about. This was precisely the idea that Anthony had hoped to get over and he felt quite pleased with himself. That was until Sheriff Bates came out of his office to see who was speechifying in the public highway and nearly tripped over one of the two corpses lying right outside his door.

'What the devil . . . ' exclaimed Bates, looking down at the obstruction which had almost sent him flying. 'What's the meaning of this?'

Anthony said, in a voice which was meant to be heard by all those standing round and watching the show, 'The meaning of it is, Sheriff, that there's been two men lynched and I brought them here so that you can give them justice.'

With that, the young man turned on his heels and walked off to where he had tethered his horse on the hitching post. He found himself facing Michael and Ezra Doolan, who had seen the commotion outside the sheriff's office and come to see what was going on. Upon seeing them, Anthony forgot about his horse and walked over to his nearest neighbours. He said, 'I'm sorry for your loss, Mr Doolan. I visited with your wife just lately and I'm truly sorry for what has befallen her. But me and my family had no part in it.'

Both the Doolans knew this to be a barefaced lie and the older of the two men said, 'I've nothing to say to you or any o' your family, leastways, not 'til my dear wife is in the ground. Then I'll be at your disposal, don't you worry about that.'

'You mean to serve me as you served Jed Stone? There's his body, over yonder by Sheriff Bates' door. You want to swear to these people,' Anthony indicated the crowd with a wave of his hand, 'that you had no part in Stone's death? Just tell them, if you will.'

This was too much for Ezra Doolan, whose hand moved towards the holster at his hip. His father's hand snaked out, grabbing his son's wrist. Then he looked Anthony straight in the eyes and said once more, 'I've nothing to say to you,' upon which, he and his son walked away, taking no further notice of either Anthony, or the bunch of people who were watching avidly, wondering if there was about to be gunplay.

Sheriff Bates was not a happy man after witnessing the exchange between young Armstrong and Doolan. He went over to where Anthony was now untying his horse and said, 'I got a crow to pluck with you, young fellow.'

'What would that be, Sheriff?'

'I don't rightly know all that's going

on between you and the Doolans, but I'll thank you not to bring it to this town. This is a peaceful place and I aim to keep it that way.'

'Are you going to investigate Jed Stone's death?'

'I don't need you to teach me my job. I know what I'm about.'

'Well, that's a mercy!' said Anthony quietly, as he adjusted the stirrup and vaulted onto the back of his horse. He didn't ride off at once, but sat there for a moment, gazing down at Brewster Bates. Then he said, 'My family don't want any trouble. You warn the Doolans to steer clear of us and we'll all be happy.' Having delivered himself of this parting shot, he set his horse trotting along Main Street, the two ponies in tow.

As he rode home, Anthony felt moderately satisfied with what he had achieved that morning. It would not do his family any good at all to be seen in the character of ruthless killers — killers of a woman, into the bargain. After all, they still had to trade in the town and continue to live in the district. His little exhibition that morning had surely been enough to sow seeds of doubt in the minds of those living in Parson's End, as to which of the two families was really the wronged party in this present dispute. With luck, people would decide that there was nothing to choose between them and just write off the short spate of killings as an aberration. That was fine; his mother, father and brothers could then live it down until it was all forgotten.

He felt a little bad about lying to Mr Doolan's face like that, after the man had suffered such a grievous loss, but that couldn't really be helped. His first loyalty was to his own kin. It was while musing in this way that he reached home, to find that everything was quiet there.

★ ★ ★

Meeting Anthony in town like that had served only to confirm Michael Doolan's suspicion that the entire Armstrong family were involved in his wife's murder. He knew nothing at all about the shooting of Seth Armstrong other than what the man's sons had been saying, and for all he knew to the contrary, the whole thing was a pack of lies. He would never now learn the truth of the matter and discover that it was his own hired man who had started this whole chain of events in motion.

As far as Doolan was concerned, all the Armstrongs were in this together, even young Anthony, who he had hitherto regarded as being innocent of involvement. Now, Michael Doolan thought it likely that the young man's visit to see his wife just a few short hours before she had been killed was part and parcel of some plan devised by Seth Armstrong. He knew now which of the brothers had actually pulled the trigger, but in his own mind, they were all culpable and every one of them would pay the price for what had been done.

It was in this grim frame of mind that Doolan reached his own home. Ezra hadn't said much on the way back from town. His father suspected, quite rightly, that his son was not wholeheartedly behind the plan that was being hatched, but he knew also that Ezra and Joe would, when it came down to it, go along with whatever their father suggested. That was what family meant.

The day before, Doolan had sent one of his hands riding over towards the New Mexico Territory. From time to time, the Doolans traded with a band of comancheros who operated thereabouts. Men of that stamp were not commonly found so far west, but this bunch had made it a little hot for themselves elsewhere and so had drifted over towards Arizona until things had cooled down a mite.

Now, although comancheros were in the usual way of things ready to engage in all types and degrees of villainy, they tended to avoid getting up to their tricks in districts where there were regular peace officers or settled communities. There was good reason for this. What might perhaps be overlooked in the wild country of New Mexico, where the only law might be a hundred miles distant, would not be tolerated where there were decent folk living. These fellows had a healthy respect for vigilance committees and the like and took good care not to hazard their necks by falling foul of a lynching party.

In this case though, matters would be quite different. They were being invited to come and stay on Doolan's land and given to understand that there would be an opportunity for looting a prosperous spread and carrying off whatever livestock, portable goods and money was to be found. In return, they needed only to help kill five men, which was, as one might say, all in a day's work for such individuals.

Davy Frobisher, the fellow that had been to carry word to the comancheros, was hanging about the yard, waiting to deliver the answer of the men he'd been to see. Frobisher was no weakling or coward, but those men had set the fear of God into him. They'd been polite enough, even friendly, but Frobisher hadn't felt like hanging around in that camp, not once he'd given his message and received the answer. He guessed that the men were well aware what effect they had upon visitors, because as he turned to ride off, he'd heard a couple of mocking chuckles. There'd been times in his life when Davy Frobisher had fought men for considerably less than laughing at him like that. He felt no inclination, though, to take affront with any of those fellows, simply urging his horse into a trot and then almost at once a canter, so anxious was he to put a bit of distance between him and those comancheros.

'Well?' said Doolan when he caught sight of Davy Frobisher. 'What's the answer?'

'They say they'll be here tomorrow afternoon. Said they're right glad to oblige you.'

Michael Doolan turned to his son and said quietly, 'Well, that about settles the business, I should say. Those men as helped us settle those fellows last night, they won't follow me much further. Bunch o' milk-sops! Those hangings was the most I can expect of 'em. Not to fret. I've had dealings with those comancheros before. They're by way of being customers of mine.'

'You want that me and Joe should take . . . Ma to the church tomorrow morning?'

'Yes, that's the idea. I'd o' liked to have those who killed her under the ground before she was herself buried, but it can't be helped. I tell you now, Seth Armstrong and his boys won't be more than a few days behind your ma in goin' underground. Mind, I think they'll be spending eternity in a less pleasant place than your ma, God rest her.'

★   ★   ★

Seth Armstrong had insisted on rising from his bed and when Anthony got back from town was walking about as though nothing had happened. Tom caught Anthony's eye and shook his head in despair. What was even worse was that their father was talking once more of riding over to the Doolans' and trying to straighten out what he called, 'this foolish misunderstanding'. It was clear that the old man wasn't about to take any heed of what Tom, Andrew and Jack said, so Anthony thought it would do no harm if he attempted to tackle things here, before they spiralled out of control. He said, 'Pa, you need to be resting. That wound's going to open up again if you're not careful.'

'Stop fussing,' said his father, 'you're like a bunch of women.'

'I'm sure Ma says the same thing. You need to take things easy for a spell. Just a week or so. Why not get back to bed and me and the others will do what's needful?'

Martha Armstrong was hovering by

the range, her face drawn with anxiety and worry. Her husband said, 'I don't rightly know what you boys have been up to to upset old Mick Doolan, but I have to make it up with him. We were always good friends. I can't think what's gone wrong.'

It sounded to Anthony, and his brothers later confirmed it, that their father had forgotten about the feud with the Doolans, which had been going for some time before this. Seth evidently had it in mind that he and Doolan were great chums and it needed only a few words together for them to settle whatever silly misunderstanding had arisen.

'Pa, things have gone too far for that,' said Anthony gently. 'His wife's dead. He's looking for revenge.'

'Susan Doolan dead?' asked his father, a look of genuine distress upon his face. 'Why that's terrible. Just terrible. All the more reason I should go see Mick. I must offer my condolences.'

It struck Anthony that short of

binding his father hand and foot, there was little they could do to stop him from embarking upon a course of action which would certainly result in his death. Cunningly, he said, 'It would be no kindness to disturb Mr Doolan at such a time. The family is in mourning, you know. Tell you what, why not wait until after the funeral, when they'll be receiving visitors again. That makes more sense.'

Even as a child, Anthony had had the knack of sweet-talking the old man and he rejoiced to see that his words were working to some effect. His father looked undecided, until Martha added her two cents worth, saying, 'The boy's right, Seth. It'd be no kindness to go there now, stirring up strife. Let it be until after the funeral.'

'Well, happen you're both right,' said Seth, 'but the second the family are receiving visitors again, that's where I'm bound. You can bet on it.'

8

The day of Susan Doolan's funeral dawned bright and clear. Shortly after dawn, Ezra and Joe harnessed up the cart and then reverently carried their mother's body out and laid it on the back of the cart, shrouded in an old sheet. It was the hell of a thing to feel the dead weight of your own mother in that way and, tough as the boys were, they both had tears in their eyes as they drove off towards Parson's End.

Anthony and his brothers agreed that the best thing was for them to stay away from town for a while. They didn't know that the funeral was being held that very afternoon, but could see that they might all be needed if their father took it into his head again to go over to the Doolans' place. Seth was sitting quietly in the parlour, but he hadn't said much that morning. It seemed to

151

Anthony that his father was even more distracted since the shooting than he had been before. Whether it was that the shock of the thing had disordered the old man's brain, he didn't know, but whereas before he had been shot, Seth had been mildly vague and forgetful, now it looked as though he'd lost his wits.

There was much that needed to be done to keep business running smoothly, but all the brothers had the same feeling; they would be better to keep close to the house and set a guard upon their parents. The day wore on in this fashion, with the close confinement wearing on the brothers' nerves and their ma fussing round the old man, who sat silent and brooding. That's how it was until the late afternoon, when Tom, Andrew and Anthony decided to ride around the property, checking that there were no strangers in the vicinity nor any sort of threat that could be detected. Jack agreed to stay and keep an eye on their parents.

As soon as the others had gone, Jack

went off to the barn for an invigorating draught of poteen. It was a damned nuisance, because Jed and Albert had made the best moonshine liquor in the Arizona Territory and Jack supposed that he would be compelled to find another supplier now or pay the ruinous prices demanded at the stores in town. The poteen tasted like nectar of the gods and he sat there for a little while, imbibing enough to tide him over 'til his brothers returned and he could come back out to the barn and settle down for a half hour or so.

Because her husband was so quiet and seeing that she had had no privacy at all to speak of, Martha Armstrong thought it might be safe to leave her husband to his own devices for five minutes while she visited the privy. She had barely settled down there, when she heard the shout of a man urging on a horse, followed by the drumming of hoof beats near at hand. When she hitched up her drawers and emerged from the outhouse, it was to see her husband galloping away bareback, in the direction of the Doolans' place.

Martha Armstrong let out a cry of anguish and then shouted for her son. Jack came out of the barn, blinking owlishly as the sunlight struck his face. He said, 'What's to do, Ma?'

'What's to do? I'll give you what's to do, you young turnip-head. Your father's just rode off, heading into Lord knows what mischief and all you can do is stand there like a . . . like I don't know what. Bestir yourself and get after him.'

'I'll saddle up. It won't take me but a minute.'

In fact it took Jack Armstrong something more than a minute to saddle up a horse and get after his father. If Seth Armstrong had been, as his wife suspected, galloping for the whole time since he left, then she figured he'd have a good three-mile lead on Jack.

When the others returned, some twenty minutes later, they agreed that their pa must have felt like a prisoner under guard. He'd bided his time and then

154

bolted just as soon as he was alone. There was no point in criticizing Jack, who Anthony guessed had been getting liquored up in the barn when their father left. The only thing to work out now was what to do for the best.

Since the shock of receiving a ball through his chest, Seth Armstrong's thoughts had been even foggier than usual. He was perfectly well aware that he tended lately to get himself into a muddle, but prided himself on being able to conceal this shortcoming from the other members of his family. Things were worse now, though, for they were watching him oddly, as though preparing to keep him prisoner. And at a time such as this, when his old friend Mick Doolan needed his support in his hour of grief. That something should have happened to Susan Doolan was a terrible business, even though he didn't really understand the ins and outs of it all.

It was a good long time since he'd ridden bareback and the feeling of the wind rushing past and the warm flanks of the horse between his legs was exhilarating. This was the way to clear the cobwebs away all right! Why, he felt ten years younger already; he should have done this months ago, when first he felt his mind becoming a little dulled. It was in this exalted frame of mind that he urged on his mount, which, setting its foot in a hole left by some burrowing animal, promptly came to a sharp halt. The beast tipped its rider forward, over its head, before somersaulting and rolling on the hapless man lying in its path.

The pain was worse than anything Seth had ever felt in the whole course of his life. He lay there, unable to breathe without the most agonizing sensation shooting through his ribs. Instinctively, Seth Armstrong was aware that he had done himself a serious mischief. It was in this helpless condition that his son Jack came upon him five minutes later.

Leaping nimbly from his horse, Jack

cried, 'Pa, what in the hell have you gone and done?'

His father groaned, attempted to speak and then, finding the effort too much for him, gave up and continued lying there, looking up at the sky. Jack examined his father and could see at once that the old man's injuries were apt to prove exceedingly serious. There was blood trickling from one ear, which was seldom a good sign, and one of his legs was twisted oddly, as though the joint were out of place.

'Jeez, what possessed you?' asked Jack in a stunned voice. 'What were you thinking of, Pa?' To see his father, always the most vigorous and sturdy of men, stretched out there, helpless and injured, was too much for Jack and a lump came to his throat. Tears of sorrow prickled at the back of his eyes and if his brothers had not come along at that moment, he would most likely have begun weeping like a woman.

Anthony and Tom reined in and then dismounted. He hoped that he was wrong, but to Anthony, it looked as though his father's injuries were likely to prove mortal, unless treated. He said in a low voice to Tom, 'You want to fetch the buckboard so that we can take him home?'

'You don't think we should take him straight to the doctor in town?' replied his brother, also speaking quietly, so that their father would not hear.

Anthony shook his head and whispered, 'Not as things are now. Suppose there was fighting? Let's get him home and one of us'll go for the sawbones.'

Tom nodded and without any further debate, mounted up and sped like the wind, back the way he had come. Walking over to his brother, Anthony said, 'You all right?'

Jack rubbed his hand over his eyes, dashing away the tears and said, 'It's the hell of a thing. My fault as well.'

'Don't say so. He would have got away from us at some stage. If not now, then when we were all sleeping. It can't be helped.'

Although he had been more than a little irritated since Anthony had returned home by his younger brother's seeming assumption of authority, Jack appreciated this reassurance and reached out to grip his brother's arm. For a moment, the two of them just stood there like that, both looking down at their father, who mercifully appeared to have lapsed into unconsciousness.

It took forever, or so it seemed to them, for Tom to arrive back with the buckboard. Tenderly, and with enormous solicitude and care, they lifted their father up and placed him carefully at back of the buckboard. Tom observed to Anthony in a quiet voice, 'It's going to be the very devil of a journey for him. There's no track to speak of and he'll be shaken all to pieces.'

'It can't be helped. Just take it as slow as you can.'

Fortunately for the injured man, he did not come to during the whole of the ride home. Even when they had reached their destination and he was once again picked up and carried, Seth Armstrong showed no sign of life, other than his stertorous breathing. As she heard the rumbling of the cartwheels, Martha ran out to see what sort of state her husband was in. When she saw his pitiful condition, her hands flew to her mouth and she gave an inarticulate moan of anguish.

After they had put their father on his bed, Anthony and Tom talked over what needed to be done next. 'One of us will have to go into town and fetch the doctor,' said Anthony. 'I don't mind which of us it is, but we'd best hurry.'

'I'll go,' said Tom. 'If Pa wakes up again, he might be fractious and he's more like to heed advice from you than he is the rest of us. Lord knows what injuries he'll cause himself if'n he tries to get out of bed in his state. You set by his bedside and I'll be as quick as I can.'

'You know it's life and death? What will you do if the doctor won't come?'

'I can be mighty takin' when I've a

mind,' said Tom, smiling mirthlessly. 'Seriously, he'll come, even if I have to bring him at gunpoint.'

At this point, Jack appeared in the doorway and said firmly, 'No, let me do it. If I'd o' set a better watch on him, happen Pa wouldn't've got away.'

After Susan's funeral, Michael Doolan and his two sons and daughters rode back home. There was no nonsense about inviting friends and neighbours back to the house for refreshments or anything of that nature. Doolan wanted to be there ready to receive the four men who were expected that very afternoon. He didn't want anybody seeing the comancheros and asking a lot of foolish questions about them. He had a shrewd idea that none of the local people would take at all kindly to him extending his hospitality to a gang of cut-throats and giving them the green light to wreak havoc and ruin upon the family and property of a man who was well respected in the area. This was the kind of thing best done quietly and about which he could express surprise and outrage once the deed was done and the men had left the vicinity of Parson's End.

The four comancheros were waiting for the Doolans when they got home. At the sight of them, here on his own property, Michael Doolan's heart almost misgave him. He'd dealt with these men pretty regularly over the last twelvemonth, but seeing them here, right near his own house, the four of them looked far more alarming than usual.

The four men were scattered around the yard in front of the Doolans' residence. Two of them were sitting on the fence surrounding the corral, smoking and chatting, while the other two were strolling round as though they owned the place. The regular hired hands didn't know what to make of the newcomers and stood at a distance, eyeing them nervously.

The leader of the band was a man called Pascal, although whether that was his given or family name, he had never said. It might even have been some sort of nickname, but nobody knew him by any other name. When he saw the Doolans approaching, he hailed them cheerfully, crying, 'Captain Doolan! You see we make it here safely. Now we have conference, you and me, no?'

Why the leader of the comancheros bestowed the rank of 'captain' upon him, was more than Michael Doolan could say, but it was what he invariably called the man whose home he had come to visit. There was more than a suspicion of mockery in the military term and Doolan wondered once more if he had done the right thing in getting these scoundrels mixed up in his personal business. One thing was for sure; if anybody could tackle the Armstrongs and make an end of them, these were the boys to do it.

'Come in the house, just the two of us and we'll make medicine,' said Doolan. 'My boys here will show your fellows where to stow their gear.'

Once they were inside, Doolan asked the other man if he wanted a drink.

This question was met with an ironic lift of the eyebrows, as though it was a mad sort of inquiry to which there could be only one sensible answer. When the two of them had glasses of whiskey in their hands, Doolan invited Pascal to be seated and without more ado said, 'I want those five men dead within twenty-four hours. There's a deal of gold in the house, as Seth Armstrong never trusted banks. There's livestock all over the place, thirty, maybe forty horses. Then there's all kinds of other stuff to be found in the house.' Doolan opened the drawer of a nearby bureau and took out a little soft leather bag. 'On top o' that, here's five hundred in gold. I take it you're in, else you wouldn't o' come traipsin' all the way here?'

'Oh yes, I am 'in' all right. Do not make yourself uneasy about that, my friend. Give me the descriptions of these men you would have dead.'

For the next five minutes, Michael Doolan sketched out a series of word portraits of his nearest neighbours; their physical appearance, mode of dress, peculiarities and so on. By the end of it, the man who called himself Pascal felt that he would be able to recognize any of the five men, should he encounter them. Not being such a one who ever saw any need for social airs and graces, Pascal tossed off the last of his whiskey and got to his feet. He said, 'The place where these men live lies to the east of here, is it not so?'

'It is.'

'Myself and another will scout round this very minute and then tomorrow we will deal with them all.'

There was nothing more to be said and so Doolan merely nodded. Pascal left the house and shortly afterwards, there was the sound of two horses riding off into the darkening evening.

* * *

Jack Armstrong was beginning to feel the strain. The shooting of his father and now this terrible accident had made him feel of a shiver. It was the culmination of all that had lately been happening, but he was afflicted with a dreadful sense of foreboding. There was nothing he could quite put his finger on, but he felt that some awful thing was about to befall them. It was all a lot of nonsense, of course. His father's declining mental powers had been noticed some months ago and although none of them spoke much about it, they all knew that their pa was no longer holding the reins, so to speak. That had created a melancholy atmosphere in their home for a while, because Seth Armstrong had always been a strong and capable man, both physically and mentally. To witness the ebbing of his powers in this way could not help but be a depressing spectacle. Above all else, Jack desired a glass or two of ardent spirits. As soon as this errand was over, he proposed to seclude himself in the barn and get drunk.

So lost in his sad thoughts was Jack,

that he didn't notice, until he was right on top of them, the two men who were sitting quietly on their horses in the gloom, watching him draw near. When he became aware of them, he said, 'A good evening to you.' He made to ride around them, but as he did so, one of the men made his horse skitter sideways into Jack's path. He reined in and said, 'Steady on there. You nearly had us collidin'. I'll thank you to move aside, I'm in somewhat of a hurry.'

'Are you, though?' asked one of the men. 'Might I be permitted to ask your name, sir?'

'My name?' asked Jack in a puzzled tone. 'Well I don't see what affair it is of yours, but I'm Jack Armstrong. And while we're on the subject, I mind that this is my family's land you're on. Happen you didn't know.'

'Oh, we knew,' said the man and then, without any further delay, he drew a pistol and shot Jack Armstrong twice in the chest. Even in death, Jack's face wore a look of mystification; his own sudden murder was the last thing he had expected that evening. His horse was near to bolting from the gunfire, but the man who had shot him rode forward and grabbed the bridle, speaking soothingly to the spooked creature.

Back at the Doolans' house, Michael was talking matters over with his sons. Ezra said, 'Pa, you sure 'bout this? I've a real, bad feeling about those fellows.'

His brother chipped in before their father could answer saying, 'Ezra's right, Pa. We evened up the score by killing those rats. We can take Jack in a few days, when his guard's down. Surely to God it ain't needful to slaughter the whole boilin' of 'em?'

Before Michael Doolan could respond to these entreaties, there was a sharp and imperious whistle from without the house. Then they heard Pascal's call for them to come out. 'I have something to show you!' he cried.

The three of them went out into the yard. The daylight had almost completely faded and the moon was rising.

Michael Doolan said, 'Well, what's to do?'

'Only this!' said Pascal and lobbed an irregularly shaped object, about the size of a large rock, in their direction. Whatever it was bounced a little and then rolled to a halt. The three Doolans peered down, not able to figure the play. Then, almost at precisely the same instant, all three realized what it was they were looking at. It was the decapitated head of Jack Armstrong.

9

Jack's sightless eyes stared up at them, the whites of them gleaming in the twilight. Ezra, who had grown up with Jack and played with him constantly as a child, gave a cry of horror. 'God almighty,' he shouted, 'what's this?'

'Down payment,' explained Pascal nonchalantly. 'How do you say? One down, four to go, no?'

It was too much for Ezra Doolan, who stumbled off, retching and gagging. Pascal watched him with amusement and remarked to his father, 'Your son is too squeamish, is it not so? I never saw a man behave so when he saw that his enemy was dead.'

The other three comancheros had wandered up and were watching the scene with evident enjoyment. It was clear that this was not the first time that their leader had had a little fun with somebody's head. One of the men said something in Spanish and Pascal replied in the same language. There were snorts of laughter, which filled Michael Doolan with disgust. He said, 'Show some respect, that's a man!'

Pascal dismounted and then walked up close to old Doolan, kicking Jack Armstrong's head to one side as he did so. Pascal said, 'Let us rightly understand each other. You engaged me to kill men. Very well. I have done so. Don't lecture me now. I won't have it.' Then he turned on his heels and the others followed him to the barn, where they would be sleeping that night.

Ezra rejoined his father and brother. When the comancheros were safely out of earshot, he said to his father, 'What have you done, Pa? What in hell have you done?' Then, without waiting for an answer, he turned and went into the house. The other two stood there for a while, neither speaking. Then Joe too followed his brother into the house, leaving his father to meditate upon where his thirst for vengeance had led him and wondering what on earth he had unleashed.

Jack had been gone for over two hours and Seth Armstrong had come to and begun to groan and cry in the most pitiable way. His wife did her best to comfort him, but it was as plain as a pikestaff that the man was in absolute agony.

'Where's Jack got to?' said his mother. 'He should've been back by now, surely?' Anthony and Andrew exchanged looks. They had both, independently, been thinking the self-same thing. Both had the same fear as well — that somehow the Doolans might have caught Jack and injured or, God forbid, even killed him.

At last, almost three hours after his brother had left, Anthony got to his feet and announced, 'I'm going out to hunt after Jack. Andrew, maybe you and Tom would stay here and be wary? Something tells me that there's trouble afoot.' His mother was in the bedroom with their father, or he would not have spoken so openly.

The night was dark, with only the thinnest crescent of moon to light the way as Anthony rode towards Parson's End. There was, he supposed, an outside chance that Jack's horse had taken a tumble in the dark and he was lying there waiting for aid, but Anthony didn't think at all that that was likely to be the case. It would be the deuce of a coincidence if two members of the family fell off their horses in that way in the space of a few hours. It was Anthony's considered opinion that his brother had been the victim of some enemy action and he could only guess at the form this might have taken.

He was no sawbones, but it was tolerably clear to Anthony that his father was unlikely to recover from whatever injuries he had received that day. There might have been an outside chance, had his pa not been weakened by being shot, but as it was, he had been ailing before that gallop had ended in disaster. Anthony had a suspicion that there was some internal mischief in the case and that maybe his horse had rolled on the man, once he had taken a tumble.

The mount that Anthony had taken was showing signs of being inexplicably spooked. The mare was breathing oddly and snuffling the air; her ears were twitching and her head shifting from side to side. This was enough to set the young man's nerves on edge and he drew his pistol and reined the horse.

'What's the matter, girl?' he asked softly. 'Somebody up ahead?' He cocked the pistol and listened carefully. He could hear nothing other than the breeze rustling a few dry leaves somewhere near at hand. Very quietly, he dismounted and stood there in the darkness for a few seconds, listening and staring into the gloom. The mare was still jittery, but as long as she was not going to be urged on, she seemed happy enough to stand there, waiting to see what would next be required of her.

It seemed to Anthony that some vague and indistinct shape lay on the ground ahead of them and that it might perhaps have been this that had spooked the mare. He could smell nothing himself, but everybody knew that the nostrils of horses were infinitely more sensitive than those of men. Perhaps she could detect some odour of corruption to which he was oblivious. So thinking, the young man strolled over to investigate.

Although the ground was parched and dry, it not having rained for above a fortnight, Anthony found that the earth beneath his feet had a sticky feel, clinging to his boots as he moved forward, as though he were walking through mud. That's blazing strange, he thought to himself. He bent down and felt the loamy soil of the track. Sure enough, it felt slippery and damp. Moving his head down in that way brought his nose closer to the ground and for a brief moment, he caught a scent which brought back for him ghastly memories. It was the metallic, faintly sweet smell of fresh blood; a lot of it. It would have been impossible to spend as much time on battlefields as Anthony had and not become perfectly familiar with that reek. No wonder the mare had dug in her heels and been reluctant to go forward. The stink of blood was the smell of danger.

Most likely it was the remains of some animal left by a predator, but there was no percentage in taking any chances. Anthony moved forward slowly towards the dark mass, his pistol ready and his ears straining all the while for any indication that he was not alone. He could hear nothing. When he reached the formless shape, he reached down a tentative hand and found to his horror that this was no animal, but the clothed body of a human being.

Although he was no smoker, Anthony had got into the habit during the war of keeping a box of lucifers about him. This proved a practical aid, even in peace-time. After all, you never knew when you might wish to light a lamp or kindle a fire. He took out the box and struck a light. To his utter disgust, he found himself gazing down at a headless body. Almost at once, he recognized the clothes that his brother Jack had been wearing when he had set off earlier for town to fetch the doctor. He might be among the least squeamish of men after his experiences during the War Between the States, but this was too much for the young man, who dropped the match and stumbled away to vomit.

Once he had emptied his stomach and wiped his mouth clean, it took Anthony less than a minute to think through his options and decide to carry on at once towards Parson's End. After all, there was nothing to be done for his brother and there was still a chance that his father's life could be saved. It was, from all that he could collect, a slender chance, but any chance is better than none at all and it could hardly be clearer that there was nothing to be done for Jack in this world.

There was, thought Anthony as he entered the outskirts of town, no profit at all to be gained from racking his brains trying to figure out who had killed his brother. He knew he could rule out the Doolans; not a one of them had the character to saw off a man's head. Old Michael Doolan might be after their blood for his wife's death, but neither he nor his sons would do such a beastly thing. Anthony fully intended to be revenged for Jack's death, but for now, he was more concerned with trying to save his father.

Old Dr Drake was sitting in the back parlour with his wife when there came a hammering at the door. 'Lordy,' said Mrs Drake, 'surely you ain't needed this time o' night? You want I should go and get rid of whoever it is? Tell 'em to wait 'til morning?'

'No, it's not that late. Let me see who it is. If it's just a case of the croup, I'll send 'em packing with a bottle of remedy.'

Dr Drake did not at first recognize

the slender young man standing on his doorstep. 'Can I help you, son?' he asked kindly. 'What's the problem?'

'You don't recall me, sir. I've not been around for a year or two.'

The old man peered into Anthony Armstrong's face and gave an exclamation of pleasure. 'Young Anthony! You find your way home again, I see. Your mother's been waiting for you these many months. What's the matter? She sick?'

'No, sir. It's my pa.' Without wasting any words, Anthony sketched out the injuries his father had received over the last few days. As he did so, Dr Drake's face grew grave and he said, 'Your pa ain't precisely what I would call a young man, you know. I'll come with you now and see what I can do, but it may be that's not a great deal.'

★　★　★

Michael Doolan was sitting with a glass of whiskey in his hand, wondering if he'd taken a wrong turn, when there was a soft knock at the door to his private study. 'Come in!' he called. Ezra seldom disturbed his father when he was here and it was only because he was deeply troubled that he did so now. He entered the small room and stood before him. 'Well,' said Mr Doolan, 'what's to do?'

'Those fellows. Them as were making sport with Jack Armstrong's head.'

'What of them?'

'You ask 'em to come here and kill the Armstrongs?'

'That's my affair, boy. You just keep clear of them and recollect that one of the Armstrongs killed your ma.'

'One of 'em. Jack's dead now. You hire them men to kill the whole boilin' of them?'

'What if I have?'

'It ain't right. You know it ain't right, Pa. My ma's death done scramble your wits. You ain't thinking straight.'

In the normal way of things, speaking so to his father would have been taking his life in his hands, but after seeing the awful spectacle of a man's head being kicked aside like a piece of garbage, Ezra knew that he couldn't hold his tongue. To his surprise, his father did not look angry; he simply continued sitting there, apparently thinking hard. At length, he said, 'Happen you're right. What would you have me do about it?'

'Call 'em off,' said his son at once. 'Send those rascals about their business and talk to Sheriff Bates. He could raise a posse to ride out to the Armstrong place and find which of the others was mixed up with Ma's death. This ain't the way, Pa.'

Once again, his father said nothing for a spell, merely staring moodily out the window. Ezra wondered if his pa was drunk or something. Then Doolan said, 'There's a good deal in what you say. Maybe I done wrong. I'm affeared, though, that it's too late to set things straight. Those boys out there won't stop now.'

'You want I should give them their

marching orders?' asked Ezra eagerly. 'You say the word, Pa. I'm not scared of those types.'

'No,' said his father, with every sign of great reluctance. 'We'll tell them together. You're right, boy. I was so ate up with hatred and grief that I didn't stop to think. Your ma would never have wanted this.' Doolan got heavily to his feet; he felt lightheaded. Maybe, he thought, I've drunk as much is as good for me. He went over to a stout closet, which stood in one corner of the room. This he opened with a key hanging from his watch-chain. Inside were stacked four carbines, which Doolan only ever brought out when he thought that there was some serious shooting to be done. He reached out one and handed it to his son. 'Where's Joe?' he asked.

'Rode off into town some quarter hour since. You want to wait 'til he gets back?'

'No, let's just deal with this now. It's cost me five hundred dollars, but better lose that money than see myself answerable for a massacre. I don't know what I was thinking.' While he was speaking, Doolan broke open a box of shiny brass cartridges and handed some to his son. Together, they loaded the rifles and then cocked them. Then the two of them left the room with Doolan leading the way to the kitchen.

Katy and Maire were cleaning the range and preparing the food for the next day. The two of them looked up, a little alarmed to see their father and brother both carrying rifles in the house. Their father said, 'You girls stay here, now. Lock that door and stay clear of the windows.'

'What's up?' asked Maire, the younger of the two. 'Is there some trouble?'

'Nothing for the two of you to fret over,' said their pa, smiling grimly. 'Just do as I bid you, now.'

It was pitch-dark outside, with only a moon as thin as a nail paring and a meagre scattering of stars to provide light as father and son walked across the yard to the barn. From within came the glow of a lamp and sound of talking and laughter. When Doolan and his son walked in, silence fell. The four comancheros were lying at their ease on bales of straw, passing round a bottle. Doolan noted with irritation that all of them were smoking cheroots. He said, just as he would to any of the other men who worked for him, 'Put those out. Anybody smoking in this here barn is liable to instant dismissal!'

A burst of laughter greeted this announcement and the man called Pascal got to his feet. There was something reptilian about the way that he uncoiled himself and rose up to his full height, almost like a rattler getting ready to strike. Very slowly, picking his way delicately across the straw-strewn floor of the barn, he advanced until his face was barely a foot from Doolan's. Then he halted and said gently, 'What would you have, Captain?'

'I'd have you and your men leave my barn. Take that money I gave you and be off with you. I want no more blood-shed.'

'Would you have it so, indeed? We should settle for your five hundred dollars and forget our plunder. Is that the way of it?'

'You listen to what my pa tells you,' said Ezra stoutly. 'He wants you off his land.'

'You gave us to believe that these Armstrongs were like to have some thousand or so dollars hidden in their house,' said Pascal, his eyes boring into those of the older man in front of him. 'Is it not so? You promised us the pick of horses, goods and money. All that in addition to the gold you would pay us. You recollect what I say, old man?'

'I changed my mind.'

'Yes? Perhaps then we change our minds. You promised us a house to loot, horses for the taking and I don't know what-all else. What if we change our minds and take these things here and not at your enemies'. How would that be?'

'Don't you think on it!' said Ezra

Doolan, beginning to feel more than a little uneasy at the course that events seemed to be taking. The comanchero leader had still not taken his eyes from those of the older man. He continued, 'Perhaps, who knows, you have more than those Armstrongs. Have they two pretty girls, as ripe as juicy plums, looking as though they have never laid with a man? No? You might have more for us than your enemies can offer.'

Hearing his sisters spoken of in this way, Ezra Doolan started forward, meaning to knock the mocking smile from the face of the man called Pascal. His father, though, shot out a hand and gripped his son's arm, holding him back. He said, 'Is that all you'll say?'

Pascal shrugged and replied, 'For now, yes. We will not be cheated. No man living has ever given us short measure and lived to boast of it. You would do well to remember that.' Then, as though he was dismissing a servant, he simply turned his back on the two Doolans and went back to where he had been relaxing with the other three men. Once he was again comfortably settled on a bale of hay, he reached into his pocket, extracted a cigarillo and, striking a lucifer on the heel of his boot, lit it carefully.

★　★　★

Dr Drake's face grew grave as he examined Seth Armstrong. Martha had refused to leave the room and Anthony stood inconspicuously in the corner, observing closely the doctor's expression. He was able to gauge from this, without any other clues, that his father's case was a poor one.

'Well,' said Mrs Armstrong anxiously, 'what's the verdict?' Her husband had lapsed into unconsciousness again and so she felt that plain speaking was possible. The doctor, though, felt a little delicacy at delivering his diagnosis in the presence of the man concerned, even if he was quite oblivious to the world around him. He said, 'Let's step into the other room, hey?'

Once they had left the bedroom, Dr Drake said, 'Martha, I got to tell you that your husband's not long for this world. He's got internal injuries; feels to me like his spleen's ruptured. You're religious; now'd be a good time to fetch a priest. I doubt he'll make it through the night.'

If Anthony had not been standing behind his mother when she received this terrible news, he had not the least doubt that she would have collapsed on the spot. As it was, he saw her swaying and was able to guide her gently to a chair. Seeing her looking so helpless and frail all but broke his heart. He said, 'Just you set here for a space, Ma.'

'What will I do, son? What'll I do without your pa?'

Leaving his mother sitting there, Anthony showed the doctor from the house, asking him, 'You think my father will be in pain?'

'I'd be surprised if he comes round again, 'fore he dies,' replied Dr Drake bluntly, 'but if he does, I can let you have something to give him. Come out with me to my horse.'

Dr Drake rooted about in a saddle-bag and fished out a small bottle, the glass of which was heavily ribbed, so that even in the dark, one knew that the contents were hazardous. He handed this to Anthony, saying, 'Give your pa a couple of spoonfuls when the pain gets too much for him.'

'What is it?'

'Laudanum.'

'Laudanum? That's opium in a solution, isn't it? I knew men in the war that became slobbering addicts to this stuff.'

'To speak plainly, boy, I don't think that your father's going to live long enough to develop a habit for laudanum. His life'll be measured in hours, nothing more.'

'What do we owe you?'

'You or one of your brothers call by when next you're in town. We'll settle up then.'

'There's truly nothing to be done?'

'With a ruptured spleen and your pa's other injuries? I'm not a miracle worker.'

After the doctor had ridden off, Anthony went in search of his mother. He found her sitting at her husband's bedside. The change in her was astounding. All his life, Anthony and his brothers had lived in awe of this woman. He recalled the story that Mrs Doolan had told him about his mother chasing into Parson's End after Jack and fetching him home again. The contrast between the woman who could have undertaken such a mission and the shrunken old lady he now saw sitting there in the gloom of the bedroom was beyond all reason. It was as though she had aged twenty years since hearing the terrible news of her husband's impending death. Anthony stooped and kissed the top of her head and then handed her the bottle of laudanum.

'Dr Drake said to give Pa a couple of spoonfuls of this if he seems in pain. It's laudanum.' Martha nodded, without replying. 'I've one or two matters that require my attention, Ma,' he told her. 'I'll be back as soon as may be.'

10

Michael Doolan knew that he'd taken a false turn in inviting those comancheros to help him wreak his vengeance, but there was little enough to be done about that now. The important thing was to protect his daughters from harm. When he and Ezra went back into the house, he said to his son, 'Take Katy and Maire into town. Don't argue 'bout it now. I want them away from here.'

'Those fellows'll hear. I shouldn't wonder if they're not watching just such a move,' said Ezra. 'I saw their faces. They got it in mind to take advantage of the girls. Maybe they're a-goin' to kill us as well, but they surely want the girls.'

'Got a better scheme in mind?' asked his father in a tone of voice that suggested that he didn't believe so for a moment.

'Pa, if I hadn't've opened fire the other night, happen Ma would still be with us. I don't think any o' the Armstrongs would've shot us. Things got out o' hand. It was my fault.'

'I thought on this,' said Doolan shortly. 'There may be somewhat in it.'

'Let me run over to the Armstrong place and ask 'em for help? They help us get rid of those villains in the barn, maybe the score'll be even.'

It wasn't a brilliant idea, but from where Michael Doolan was standing, there didn't look to be a better one on offer. He'd been a damned fool to hire those bandits and if it came to shooting, then he and his sons would like as not be outgunned. Besides which, there were his daughters to think of. He said, 'Well, if you're going, then go. Don't stand here gossiping like a woman. Don't saddle up. Go on foot. Those rogues'll hear any hoof beats leaving here.'

So it was that about an hour and a half later Anthony Armstrong, who had armed himself to the teeth with a view to avenging his brother Jack's killing and the mutilation of his body, saw a figure silhouetted on the ridge above his family's house. He was standing talking to Andrew, discussing his plans, when he chanced to look up and see somebody on foot, making his way towards them.

Now although he couldn't imagine any of the Doolans, no matter how grave the supposed provocation, doing something as beastly as slicing off a man's head, it was to the Doolans that Anthony had been intending to go first in order to begin his investigations. Since the figure which came briefly into sight as it crested the ridge was evidently coming from that direction, it struck both Anthony and Andrew as being a smart move to lay in wait and ambush whoever was coming their way. With a few muttered words between them, they slipped behind the low stone wall which separated the house from the yard. So it was that when Ezra Doolan was within twenty yards of the Armstrong place, two shadowy figures reared up out of the darkness and he heard the sharp, metallic click of weapons being cocked.

'I mean you all no harm,' said Ezra. 'I'm coming peaceable, like.'

'Then just keep your hands still and don't go making any sudden movements,' said Anthony. 'Just so we understand each other.'

'Anthony, I got no cause for a quarrel with you.'

'What about me, Ezra?' enquired Andrew. 'You after me?'

'I ain't after anybody. You're in danger and so are we. I come to ask your aid, but it's in your own interests.'

'How's that?' asked Anthony. 'You know aught about my brother Jack?'

Ezra was glad that the darkness shielded him from plain view, for at the mention of Jack, he found himself blushing with guilt. He said, 'You boys going to hold me at gunpoint, or can we go in the house to talk? Maybe we don't have a heap o' time to spare.'

'Come on into the house, then,' said Anthony, 'but keep your voice hushed.

My pa's ailing and like to die.'

'I'm real sorry to hear it,' replied Ezra. 'Afore this trouble I always got on right well with your father. He's a good man.'

Once they were seated at the kitchen table, Ezra set out enough of the facts to indicate the danger that the Armstrongs were in. He described the nature of the comancheros and his belief that they would stop at nothing. Andrew was very far from pleased to hear about this and said angrily, 'Your father hired these men to kill us and now you're here beggin' our aid to send them away again? That makes strange listenin'! You got a rare nerve coming to us now. So it was them as killed our Jack, that right?'

'You want straight talkin',' said Ezra Doolan, 'then your precious brother killed my ma. You know that's true. We both lost somebody. You help us get those men away and we'll call a halt to this madness.'

There was dead silence for a while after Ezra delivered himself of this proposal. Both Anthony and his brother could see that unless they went along with Ezra's plan, then the most likely consequence would be some sort of range war, which would most likely not end until nearly all of them were dead. Such things had been known before. Once killing for killing began, things soon spiralled out of control. Then again, if what Ezra said was true, then they had four ruthless killers to contend with and their mother there in the house with their father dying. Neither of them wanted their father's death to be marked with gunplay around the place.

At length, Anthony said, 'Your father agrees to this? That my brother evens out your ma's death, God rest her?'

'He's been distracted with the loss of our ma. When he comes to himself he will. He knows all this hiring of those man-killers has been a piece of foolishness.'

Turning to his brother, Anthony said, 'What d'you say? You want to go with this?'

'We don't have another choice,' said Andrew grimly. 'We carry on down this road, we're all goin' to wind up dead and those killers picking over our corpses into the bargain.'

Before setting off, they hunted out Tom, who was in their parents' room, watching over them. It was agreed that one of them at least had best stay to guard the old folks and Tom said that he would undertake that task.

'Well I came on foot,' said Ezra, 'and I reckon we should get back as speedy as can be.'

*　*　*

Pascal and his compadres were no strangers to strong liquor. Some men grow more mellow and thoughtful after a drink or two; others become boisterous and excited. There are those, though, who merely become meaner and more dangerous when in their cups. This was the case with the four comancheros in the Doolans' barn.

They fully intended to do as they had agreed and kill all the Armstrongs the next day, but tonight they had something else on their minds. That something was the two Doolan girls; Katy and Maire.

Pascal had seen the girls soon after arriving, when they were hanging out washing. Now, he could not rid his mind of them. It was like that sometimes, especially when he hadn't had a woman for a while. The other three had also caught the scent of young prey and were eager to join their boss in the hunt. In the normal way of things, these men took great care to avoid anything that might look like rape when they were in a town. There was no crime regarded with more loathing and detestation by the average citizen and taking a girl by force was the quickest way of guaranteeing that a posse would be raised in next to no time. But in an out-of-the-way spot like this, the case was altered. They might be able to kill the man who had hired them, rob him

199

as well as their intended victims and then have the girls as well.

After sending his daughters upstairs, with strict instructions to lock themselves in their room and pull the furniture against the door, Michael Doolan checked that both the front and back doors to the house were locked. There was no telling what time Joe would return from town, nor yet what sort of a response Ezra would meet with from the Armstrongs. There was nothing else to do but wait.

Doolan turned down the lamps, so that he had just enough light that he wouldn't stumble over in the darkness, but not enough to provide a good view of him from outside the house. He'd no real reason to think that the men he had engaged were going to mount an assault on his home, but there was a funny little tingling at the back of his neck, which told him that danger was near.

'What say you?' asked Pascal of his three companions. 'You want those Yankee girls?'

'How so?'

'Why, we kill the old man and his son, then take them. Good pickings in the house too, perhaps.'

Slowly, grins appeared on the faces of Pascal's men. Without saying a word more, they all four got to their feet and picked up their rifles.

The first that the Doolan girls knew of anything untoward was the sound of splintering glass, followed by a fusillade of shots. Then there was dead silence. They went over to the door that they had barricaded as best they were able and strained to see if anything could be heard. There was nothing. Both had hoped to hear their father's rough voice, assuring them that everything was all right.

Over in the bunkhouse in which three men who worked for the Doolans were staying, the sound of shooting could be faintly heard. The bunkhouse was the best part of a mile from the big house; Michael Doolan valued his privacy. That being the case, it was not immediately apparent to the men lounging around in the hut and playing poker for matches, just exactly from which direction the shots had been fired. Since there was no more gunfire, they all three of them decided that it was none of their affair and continued with their game.

Neither Anthony nor Andrew felt all that much inclined to chat with Ezra as they rode over to his house. The events of the last few days were still too raw. Not only that, but they both entertained the suspicion at the backs of their minds that perhaps they were being led into a trap. For that reason, without making too much fuss about it, they both contrived to see that Ezra rode so close to them that any man hoping to take a shot in their direction would not be sure of hitting them rather than Ezra Doolan. If Ezra knew that they did not altogether trust him, he gave no outward sign of it.

When the handle of their bedroom door turned, both Katy and Maire gave muffled gasps. Summoning up all her courage, Katy called out in a quavering and unsteady voice, 'Who's there? Is that you, Pa?'

There was a low chuckle and then a man's voice said, 'Your pa ain't able to speak just now. You two had best open this door before we break it down.'

A smoother, almost silky voice said, 'Come now, young ladies. My friends and I are likely to grow angry if you keep this up. You wouldn't like us when we get angry, of that I do assure you.'

The two girls stared at each other in dumb terror. Then there was a tremendous crash as somebody kicked the door. This initial bang was followed by a series of crashes, which sounded as though a chair or something was being swung at the door, which was in fact just what was happening in the passage outside the bedroom.

Two or three minutes after the three men had set off for the Doolans' house, there came the sound of gunfire, right ahead of them in the direction they were travelling. They had already been moving at a brisk canter, but when he heard the shots, Ezra Doolan spurred his mount on into a gallop. In keeping with their unspoken agreement to stick close by him, the other two men followed suit and so the three of them raced onwards.

The door to the Doolan sisters' bedroom was a stout one and the lock not likely to give in a hurry. The bureau and washstand that Katy and Maire had managed to maneouvre against it provided another layer of safety. Batter away at the two-inch thick oak as they might, the door remained closed against them. Being positioned as it was in a narrow passageway meant that none of the four men could charge at it and hope that their weight would burst it open. It was awkward enough trying to kick against it in the enclosed space. Pascal had tried swinging a wooden jardinière against the door, but that had splintered, with no discernible effect upon the door. The comancheros were becoming frustrated and angry, knowing what tempting morsels were waiting just a few feet away. It was while they were standing baffled, that the sound of a bunch of horses heading their way came to them. With the owner of the house lying dead downstairs, they decided that they had best see who was arriving in such haste.

As Ezra Doolan and the two Armstrongs rode up, they saw that only one room in the house was ablaze with light. 'That's my sisters' room,' said Ezra. 'Lord knows why the rest of the place is so dark. And there's a window broke, there at the front.

'Something's amiss, that's for sure!' said Anthony. He scanned the darkened windows of the Doolans' house, searching for any sign of movement. He still didn't entirely trust the man to whose aid he and his brother were riding. It was true that he and Ezra had been good friends once, but much had changed since those days. He'd no idea what the man was like now, nor what game he might be playing.

They were no kind of cowards, but with a bunch of unknown riders approaching from the front of the house the best place to be, from the point of view of Pascal and his friends, was at the back. They knew each other so well, that only a whispered word or two was sufficient to set them to their allotted positions. By the time they had slipped down the stairs and moved into the kitchen, the sound of hoof beats had altogether ceased and there was dead quiet outside. Whoever was out there was seemingly watching and waiting. Friendly visitors would surely have called a cheery greeting by now or perhaps knocked on the door. The silence boded ill and when once they had unlocked the back door in the kitchen, the men split up, with two each going round either side of the house to spy out what was happening and who was there. They were keenly aware that the earlier shooting might have caused men to come running to aid the old man.

Anthony had slipped from his horse

and now made his way to the front door. By the time he reached it, his pistol was in his hand; cocked, ready and raised. The door was locked and it struck him that with the lamps dimmed in that way, somebody might be lying in wait inside the house, keeping the light low so as not to spoil their night vision. That being so, he decided to move round to the side, where there were fewer windows. He was aware of his brother Andrew and Ezra Doolan dismounting and readying themselves for action.

Unless Ezra was more devious and crooked than any man Anthony had ever met in his life, then he was as puzzled as the Armstrong brothers as to what the play might be. There was still no sign of life in the house. Taking a chance, Anthony leaned through the shattered window and saw at once Michael Doolan lying dead, a pool of blood surrounding his shattered head. From the look of him, he had stopped several bullets in his head and at least one clean through the middle of his chest. Whoever killed the old man had been well versed in both marksmanship and ruthlessness. He withdrew his head and then began moving, silently as a cat, to the side of the house.

It was the fact that he had his own weapon already levelled that saved Anthony Armstrong's life. He reached the corner of the house at just precisely the same moment that two of Pascal's men arrived from the other direction. They had their pistols in their hands but their hands were hanging loose at their sides. It was a lapse of attention of which those men would not normally be guilty. It was only that they were now in civilized country that made them a little more relaxed and less apprehensive than was the case when they were on the scout around the wild country near Palo Duro.

Anthony Armstrong sized up the situation in a fraction of a second and even as the two men were raising their pistols, he fired first at one and then the other. His first two bullets, carelessly aimed for speed, took them both in their chests, but rather than take any chances, he followed these up with more careful shots; one in the head for each man.

Ezra Doolan had his own pistol out and Andrew had pulled his rifle from the scabbard at front of his saddle. He was just bringing it up to cover any target that might present itself, when the slightest flicker of movement to the left of the house caught his eye. He shouted a warning to his brother, who was now moving along the front of the house again, heading for the other side, just in case there were other men to tackle. At the back of his mind, Anthony was worried that the two men he had killed had been part of a flanking maneouvre and that another enemy might be coming from behind him. When Andrew called out, Anthony dropped at once to the ground. This saved his life, because the man known as Pascal had been drawing down on him and fired just as Anthony went down. Pascal had no opportunity to take more time over a second shot, because Andrew fired at him. Andrew Armstrong, however, was no more than a fair to middling shot and the ball passed over Pascal's head and shattered a window. The comanchero's response was swift and deadly. He fired back at once, hitting Andrew in the fleshy part of his upper arm.

Ezra was a little slow in catching up with the action, but when he did, he tipped the balance against the men who had, unknown yet to him, killed his father. While Pascal was exchanging shots with Andrew Armstrong, Ezra took careful aim and killed Pascal's companion. Pascal himself returned fire, hitting the horse that Ezra had been riding. Then Anthony settled the matter by firing twice at the leader of the comancheros. His first bullet took Pascal in the chest; his second was as neat a head shot as one could ever hope to see, taking Pascal smack-bang between the eyes. He stood there for a second, before crashing to the ground like a felled oak.

The silence which followed the brief gunfight was broken by Katy Doolan throwing up the window and crying down to her brother, 'You settled 'em, Ezra?'

'Yeah, I reckon. You and Maire all right?'

'We are. But I'm affeared for Pa . . . '

Anthony had by this time got to his feet and before checking that all the men they had been up against were really dead, went over to see how Ezra and Andrew had fared. He was alarmed to see the blood-soaked sleeve of his brother's shirt. 'How bad is it?' he said in a low and concerned voice.

'Well,' said Andrew, 'I'm bleeding like a stuck hog, but it's only in the muscle, leastways so I think. I had worse last fall when I fell out the barn and a nail tore me. I'll live.'

'These the fellows your pa hired?' asked Anthony.

Ezra walked over to the corpses and turned their faces to him with the tip of his boot. He said, 'Yes, they're the bastards.'

Feeling that there was no point in dressing it up with fancy words, Anthony said, 'Well then, they've done for your father too. He's lying dead under that window, there on the right.'

'Ah shit, no!' exclaimed Ezra, his face suddenly twisting with grief. 'That's the hell of a thing. Don't tell the girls, Anthony. I reckon that's my job.'

11

Despite his own family's misfortunes, such as the impending death of his father, Anthony felt sorry for Ezra and his sisters. They, after all, had lost both parents in a matter of days. When Katy came downstairs, Anthony was struck by her appearance. Her hair was that same flaming red as her mother's had been, and she had filled out a little since he had last seen her in the late summer of 1865. When the sisters learned of their father's death, they were inconsolable with grief and Anthony thought that it might be in poor taste to try to renew his acquaintance just yet a while with the girl he held such a torch for.

After binding up Andrews arm as best he could there, Anthony thought it would be decent of them to withdraw and leave Ezra and his sisters to their mourning. It was at this point that three men rode up with a thunder of hoofs and after reining in, demanded that Anthony and Andrew throw down their weapons.

After besting the four comancheros, it was something of a shock to discover that the fighting might not yet be over. Fortunately, Ezra handled the situation firmly, saying to the newcomers, 'Put up your guns, you damned fools. These men are friends of mine.'

'We heard shootin',' explained one of the men. 'Second lot we heard tonight and thought as we might be needed.'

'It's good of you boys to come here like this and I'm right grateful,' declared Ezra, 'but we've dealt with the trouble.'

One of the riders who had come riding from the bunkhouse looked over to the house and saw the corpses lying where they had been killed. He said, 'What's to do? I thought your pa had hired guns. They didn't come to your aid?'

'That's them lying there,' said Ezra briefly. 'Me and these fellows had a little misunderstanding with them.'

The man gave a low whistle. 'You killed 'em all? Won't your pa be vexed 'bout that?'

Not feeling called upon to set out all his family business just then, Ezra contented himself with saying, 'Like I say, I'm grateful to you all for coming by, but we won't keep you any longer now. Thanks again.'

Taking the hint, the men left. Anthony and Andrew mounted up and Ezra came over to them. He said, 'What's happened before this night is finished with. But I tell you boys now, I'm eternally grateful as you both consented to ride out here with me. It won't be forgot. Give my regards to your ma and pa and tell 'em as things are going to be different now.'

The brothers rode home at a leisurely trot, Andrew not wanting to jolt his injured arm about over much. When once they had taken their leave of Ezra and were out of earshot, Anthony remarked, 'Well things didn't take the turn I expected tonight and that's a fact.'

'You're the hell of a shot with a pistol,' said his brother. 'Pa said that you would be, after the war and all, but I never saw the like.'

'It was close-range work,' said Anthony dismissively. 'You couldn't have missed either at that distance.'

'It ain't just the matter of not missing,' Andrew said shrewdly. 'It was the speed of the thing. You shot those two men down quick as blinking. Suppose they'd meant us no harm? You never even stopped to parley, nor nothing. Just killed 'em dead.'

'It was life and death for us. I killed men before by mistake; it happens when you live by your gun.'

'I couldn't have done it.'

Anthony said nothing for a space and then observed, 'I wonder how long this sweet new friendship'll last with the Doolans?'

'We always got on well enough 'til Pa fell out with Mr Doolan. I got no quarrel with Ezra and Joe.'

It was good to get back to their own house, although as they drew nigh to it, both men recollected that their father was probably at the point of death. Then too, there was Jack's death, which neither of them, in all the action that night, had yet had time to come to terms with. They turned out the horses after untacking them and then went to see how things were.

Tom was sitting in the kitchen. He said, 'Ma chased me out and told me that she wanted some time by her own self with Pa. I been sitting here pretty well since you fellows left.'

'I'm going to look in on Pa before I turn in,' said Anthony. 'I'll see you both in the morning.'

There was no response to his tentative tapping on his parents' bedroom door and so, very carefully, lest they were both asleep, Anthony eased open the door and peeked around it. His mother had seemingly fallen asleep while watching over her husband. She was lying, sprawled across the bed, her arms around her husband. Anthony paused for a moment to drink in the scene. Despite the tragedy of the thing, with his father likely to die before too much longer, there was something touching about the tableau. He had not the least doubt that his mother and father both loved each other now as much as they had over thirty years ago, when first they had met.

It was a pity to disrupt such a charming arrangement, but it struck Anthony that his mother would benefit from a proper night's sleep and that she would feel like the Devil tomorrow, if she spent the night like that, stretched awkwardly across the bed. He accordingly entered the room quietly and touched his mother on the shoulder, hoping to awaken her. There was no response and it was at that same moment that he was aware that his father's chest was not rising and falling. Anthony reached out his hand and found that his father was so cool to the touch that he was without doubt dead.

'That's the hell of a thing!' he muttered softly, wondering how he was going to be able to wake his mother up to deliver this devastating piece of news. He need not have worried, though, because when he shook his mother's shoulder a little more firmly, he noticed that her entire body moved, as though she were rigid and not merely relaxed in sleep. He bent down and laid a hand on her brow. To his horror, he found that she too was stone dead.

Anthony's first thought was that his mother's heart had stopped beating at the self-same moment that her husband's had given up, but even as he entertained this romantic idea, he knew that it was a lot of hooey. The human heart is a physical object, which obeys the laws of nature and when one stops beating, there is usually a practical explanation. So it proved in the present case, because when he bent down to kiss his mother's forehead, he detected at once the sweet, pungent and unmistakable odour of laudanum. A brief search of the floor beneath her chair revealed the bottle that Dr Drake had given him earlier that evening. It was perfectly empty.

From the kitchen came the voices of Andrew and Tom. Anthony knew that he would have to decide how much to tell his brothers about this. There was also the question of how to present the situation in the bedroom here to others outside the family circle.

Martha Armstrong had been a God-fearing and devout woman, whose guidance was the Good Book. Yet it was clear as daylight what had happened in the absence of he and his brothers. His father had breathed his last and as soon as she knew it, Martha Armstrong had swallowed the entire contents of the bottle of laudanum in the well-founded hope that it would prove a lethal dose. For her to have taken the awful step of self-destruction, was to Anthony a sign of how deeply she had loved her husband. Life without him had presented such an appalling prospect, that she had preferred to ignore the teaching of both church and scripture in order to bring her own life to an early close. Well, he for one did not blame her for that. Nevertheless, there were those who would and all else apart, there'd be no burying of her in consecrated ground if the minister ever found out that she was a suicide. That in turn would mean that she would not be able to be interred at her husband's side and that was a thing which was not to be thought of for a moment.

It would only be fitting to tell his brothers this very night about the death of their parents and they too might be a little shocked to think that their own mother had killed herself. Almost without thinking, Anthony slipped the empty physic bottle into his pocket and went downstairs to the kitchen to tell his brothers that their pa had died and that their mother's heart must given in at about the same moment. It was a touching little fairy tale which would harm nobody, comfort everybody and ensure that they could give their mother a fitting burial.

A week later, the joint funerals of Martha Armstrong, her husband Seth and their son Jack were held in Parson's End. In light of the feud between the Armstrongs and the Doolans, about which every person in town knew, it came as a shock to see that all four of the Doolan children who were living out at the house, were present to pay their respects to Mr and Mrs Armstrong and their boy. It was known in town that Jack Armstrong's head had somehow become detached from his body, but there was no indication of how this had occurred and Sheriff Bates had been unable to establish the facts of the case. His job had been made no easier by the quiet disposal of the corpses of the four comancheros which the Armstrong and Doolan boys had undertaken together the night after the shootout. All the men had been buried in shallow graves up in the hills, with all identifying marks removed from their belongings.

Later on the same day that the three Armstrongs had been buried, old Michael Doolan was laid to rest in the same burying ground. The Armstrongs attended that service, condoling afterwards with the children of the man whom most in Parson's End had thought to be their mortal enemy. It was not forgotten that Susan Doolan herself had died violently, nor that young Anthony had unceremoniously dumped two lynched men on Sheriff Bates' very doorstep. Seven deaths in less than a week was no common occurrence and there were many raised eyebrows. Try as he might, Brewster Bates never quite got to the bottom of the matter, despite having his own suspicions. The story of some mysterious gunman riding out of the night and shooting down Michael Doolan as he stood at the window of his house did not sound a very plausible one to the sheriff. Still, there it was; the Armstrongs and Doolans had seemingly buried the hatchet and backed each other up to the hilt on this tale.

Whether or no, the two families seemed to be on amicable terms now and none of the people living in town felt inclined to ask any questions about the recent events. It was also observed that Anthony, who from his dress looked as though he were contemplating the taking of holy orders, spent a good deal of time after the two funerals talking to young Katy Doolan.

Two weeks passed and Anthony showed no inclination to return to Massachusetts. Ezra, Joe, Andrew and Tom had, after a decent period of mourning, seemed inclined to team up and work together, rather than against each other. They had always been good friends before their fathers had fallen out and there was now no reason for them not to mend fences.

At breakfast one day, Andrew said casually to his younger brother, 'I reckon you'll be getting back to that fancy school of yours soon?'

Anthony shrugged. 'I'm going over to the Doolans' this morning. Then we'll see.'

'You'll not find Ezra or Joe there,' remarked Tom. 'We're meeting 'em in town to see about some stock.'

Andrew guffawed at this and said, 'He ain't goin' for to see the boys, you lunkhead!'

'Well there's only Katy and Maire there — ' Then he caught his brother's drift and a broad grin split his face. He said, 'Don't tell me you're courtin', Anthony?'

A little nettled, Anthony muttered something to the effect that it would be a fine thing if folk could just mind their own damned business.

It was late afternoon before Anthony Armstrong rode back from the Doolan place. His brothers and the Doolan boys were still about some business or other involving livestock. Anthony supposed that he would have to find out the ins and outs of it all before much longer. He'd an idea that things could be arranged a good deal better in a business sense if somebody with a little book-learning took a hand in it. Making a living out of horse stealing was just sheer madness. Not that he proposed to push himself forward, but if the two families, as looked likely, were to work together, then somebody had better take charge of the paperwork end of the enterprise. He reined in the mare a quarter mile from the house and surveyed the scene tranquilly.

The afternoon sun shone on a pleasing and peaceful vista. It struck Anthony that it was now certain that the two families would be stuck with each other for good or ill. He and Katy Doolan had in the last week or so rekindled the spark between them. That afternoon, he had tentatively voiced his feelings, to find that Katy felt the very same way and had been hoping that Anthony would speak out. Now that he had done so, there was no question of returning to Harvard and it only remained to apprise his brothers of the state of play.

They say that it's an ill wind that blows nobody any good and although the recent weeks had been filled with drama and tragedy, it seemed to Anthony that some good had come out of it all, at least for him personally. He spurred on the mare and rode on to the house. There was a lot to do.

We do hope that you have enjoyed reading this large print book.

Did you know that all of our titles are available for purchase?

We publish a wide range of high quality large print books including:
Romances, Mysteries, Classics
General Fiction
Non Fiction and Westerns

Special interest titles available in large print are:
The Little Oxford Dictionary
Music Book, Song Book
Hymn Book, Service Book

Also available from us courtesy of Oxford University Press:
Young Readers' Dictionary
(large print edition)
Young Readers' Thesaurus
(large print edition)

For further information or a free brochure, please contact us at:
Ulverscroft Large Print Books Ltd.,
The Green, Bradgate Road, Anstey,
Leicester, LE7 7FU, England.
Tel: (00 44) **0116 236 4325**
Fax: (00 44) **0116 234 0205**

Other titles in the
Linford Western Library:

THE BADMAN'S DAUGHTER

Terry James

When Daniel Cliff arrives in Ranch Town, he discovers the settlement is caught in the stranglehold of a brutal tyrant, and refuses to take sides. That is until the spirited Charlotte 'Charlie' Wells, heir to the Crooked-W ranch, crosses his path. When she offers him the chance to help her right the wrongs being rained down on the town, he has no qualms about using her troubles to further his own ambitions. However, Charlie is no pawn in a man's game — and nobody is going to stand in her way . . .

KILL THE TIN STAR!

Jake Henry

They warned Savage not to take the short cut through Dead Man's Gulch. Too many Apaches, they said. The warning, however, failed to mention anything about Craig and Bobby Vandal. Father and son. One a cold killer, the other prepared to do anything for his boy. When Savage arrives in the Gulch, the local sheriff has Bobby locked up on a murder charge. Craig swears his son will never hang. Before long, a deputy's badge is pinned to Savage's chest, and he holds a smoking-hot Winchester in his hands . . .

BUFFALO WOLF

Colin Bainbridge

On his way out to the diggings, fate throws John Creed together with Polly Chantry, whose wagon he frees from the mud. At the diggings they meet with Timber Wolf Flynn and his Sauk wife, White Fawn, but there is no sign of Polly's father, for whom she has been searching. The two of them set out on a double mission: to find Polly's father, and acquire weapons to help the prospectors fight off the increasing threat from outlaws. Their quest leads them into the mountains, and to a frightening discovery . . .

100 GOLDEN EAGLES FOR IRON EYES

Rory Black

Bounty hunter Iron Eyes is heading south to Mexico in search of outlaws Bodine and Walters, but is himself being hunted down by his erstwhile sweetheart Squirrel Sally. Then Iron Eyes learns that Sally has been kidnapped by landowner Don Jose Fernandez, and rushes to her aid. But Sally, Iron Eyes and the outlaws are all just pawns in a much larger game, with an enemy more deadly than they can imagine — and Iron Eyes has to use all his courage and skill to survive.